D0839585

BOOKS BY BRENDA S. ANDERSON

THE POTTER'S HOUSE BOOKS

Long Way Home
Place Called Home
(Coming September 2018)
Home Another Way
(Coming February 2019)

WHERE THE HEART IS SERIES

Risking Love
Capturing Beauty
Planting Hope

COMING HOME SERIES

Pieces of Granite
Chain of Mercy
Memory Box Secrets
Hungry for Home

THE POTTER'S HOUSE BOOKS, BOOK 4

Long Way Home

A NOVELLA

VIVANT
PRESS

Minneapolis, Minnesota

Vivant Press
Long Way Home
Copyright © 2018
Brenda S. Anderson

ISBN-13: 978-0-9862147-7-6

Scriptures taken from the Holy Bible, New International Version®, NIV®. Copyright © 1973, 1978, 1984, 2011 by Biblica, Inc.™ Used by permission of Zondervan. All rights reserved worldwide. www.zondervan.com The "NIV" and "New International Version" are trademarks registered in the United States Patent and Trademark Office by Biblica, Inc.™

This novel is a work of fiction. Names, characters, places, and incidents either are the product of the author's imagination or are used fictitiously. Any resemblance to actual events, locales, organizations, or persons living or dead is entirely coincidental and beyond the intent of either the author or the publisher.

Front Cover Design by T.K. Chapin
Back Cover Design by Think Cap Studios

Printed in the United States of America

18 19 20 21 22 23 24   7 6 5 4 3 2 1

Note from the Author

The 21 books that form **The Potter's House Books** series are linked by the theme of Hope, Redemption, and Second Chances. They are all stand-alone books and can be read in any order. Books will become progressively available beginning March 27, 2018.

Book 1: **The Homecoming** by Juliette Duncan

Book 2: **When it Rains** by T.K. Chapin

Book 3: **Heart Unbroken** by Alexa Verde

Book 4: **Long Way Home** by Brenda S. Anderson

Book 5: **Promises Renewed** by Mary Manners

Book 6: **A Vow Redeemed** by Kristen M. Fraser

Book 7: **Restoring Faith** by Marion Ueckermann

Books 8 – 21: *to be advised*

Visit **www.PottersHouseBooks.com** for updates on the latest releases.

To my daughter, Sarah

God couldn't have blessed me with a
more amazing daughter!
Thank you for making motherhood look good on me.

You must go on adventures
to find out where you belong.

~ Sue Fitzmaurice ~

Chapter One

eneath the words "May love always be our home" stenciled on the living room wall, Lauren Bauman's piano had at last found its home. Now it was time for her to do the same, and today the journey to that home would finally begin. She couldn't wait to take off on the road trip, even if it was with her *sort-of* brother.

She ran her fingers over the walnut finish on the forty-year-old Yamaha that had been her mom's prize possession. It still maintained the showroom floor sheen, but after its most recent move, it likely wouldn't sound as beautiful as it looked. She sat on the bench, splayed her fingers over the keys, and played the first measures of Beethoven's "Fur Elise," one of her mom's favorite pieces. No doubt, she would be pleased with the Yamaha's new residence, a place called Our Home where formerly-homeless young adults were loved and learned how to live.

But a few measures of the song were all Lauren's ears could take. The move from Brainerd to this northern Minneapolis suburb had wreaked havoc on the tuning, creating a warped, almost haunted tone. Later this week though, a master piano tuner would mold those notes back into shape, and beautiful music would flow from the keys once again.

A door slammed behind Lauren and she jerked her hands from the keyboard. Even after these past four years of living with the Brooks family, she was still uncomfortable playing for anyone other than God.

"How's it sound?" Nate whipped past her to the kitchen. He was always packing away food, yet he didn't gain an ounce. Life was unfair.

She slid the keylid over the ivories and joined Nate at the kitchen island, a half-eaten apple in his hand. "Right now, it sounds a lot like a musician on a wavy lake. It didn't appreciate the ride down, but after the tuner comes, it'll be all ready for the residents to take lessons."

"Hmm." Nate bit into the apple then spoke with his mouth full. It didn't matter that his mom had constantly chastised him for the action. "Mom and Dad are gonna miss the music."

"You think so?" They'd rarely mentioned her music, but then she'd seldom played the piano when they were around.

He shrugged and wiped an arm across his chin. "Well, mostly they're gonna miss you. And Jaclyn, she's gone all drama queen on us with her big 'sister'"—he made air quotes— "moving away from home."

But the Brooks' house had never been Lauren's home. Not really. She stared out the patio doors at a backyard bursting with new spring life. "It's time." Time for her to make her own home. The Brooks' place had just been where she'd temporarily stored what little she owned until she graduated from college. She would be forever grateful to Nate's family for taking her in after her dad died and letting her stay until now. With college behind her, and a job waiting in New York, it was time for her to blossom.

Nate set down his apple and touched her arm, drawing her attention from God's artwork beyond the patio doors. "You're gonna do amazing things, Lauren."

"Thanks." Still, after four-plus years, she couldn't come up with more than one-word sentences when talking with Nate, although their relationship had drastically changed from adversarial to one of respect. Nowadays he was the first to stand up for her and believe in her like a true big brother would.

And now he was helping her move twelve hundred-plus miles across country in an old school bus Nate and a friend had converted into an RV, with dreams of road-tripping around the country. This would be The Draken's maiden voyage, so naturally they had to throw in some fun stops along the way. With three weeks until her job started, they had a lot of time to enjoy the road trip. She couldn't wait to get going!

Lauren pushed away from the island. "You ready?" The Draken was already packed with her few belongings. Without a place to call her own these past four years, accumulating things hadn't made sense. Now she was grateful for that wisdom.

"Almost." Nate wiped a napkin across his face and left it on the counter. She shook her head, holding in a chuckle.

Some things never changed. "I need to talk with Nancy first." He nodded toward the office where Our Home's administrator was bunkered in for month-end work. "This involves you too." His voice sounded way too somber.

What was up with that?

With nerves tingling in her hands, she followed him to the office. He knocked on the French doors.

Nancy looked up from her computer, grinned, and waved them in. "About to take off?"

Nate held a chair for Lauren, then sat beside her. "There's something I need to ask first."

Uh-oh. Dread churned in her stomach. What could possibly be wrong? The Our Home organization had nothing to do with their trip.

Nancy closed her laptop. "What's on your mind, Nathan?"

"I, uh, well you know it's a long drive from here to New York."

She didn't comment but raised her eyebrows.

"And I . . . " His fingers drummed out a rapid beat on his thighs. "So I have someone to keep me company on the way home, I'd like to ask Jet to come with us."

Who was Jet? Nate had never mentioned him before. With Nate bringing the request before Nancy, it made sense that Jet was part of Our Home's family.

Nancy took in a breath and folded her hands on her desk. This Jet guy must be trouble. "You're free to ask, and he's free to leave."

"I know that, but I wanted to get your impression first."

Nancy's mouth drew into a grim line, and she directed her gaze to Lauren. "Do you know Jet?"

She shook her head. "He lives here, I assume?"

"For the past month." Nancy nodded toward Nate and shook her head. "One of his strays."

No surprise there. To help fund college, Nate had become an Uber driver, which he then turned into a ministry of sorts. He was always bringing strangers to Our Home, many of whom had been pretty jagged around their emotional edges. Time spent here usually smoothed those edges.

So, if Nate thought this Jet would be a good fit for their road trip, who was she to argue? She'd learned to trust his judgment.

Lauren looked directly at Nate, affirming him. "I wouldn't have a problem with it." Well, maybe that was a little lie. Adjusting to strangers always took time. Yes, she'd lost some of the insecurity of her high school years, but not all of it.

Perhaps this was one of those God-provided challenges. Being stuck in a vehicle with a stranger on a long road trip was one way to face those insecurities dead-on. Being shy wouldn't be an option. Clutching her hands in her lap, she turned her attention to Nancy. "Nate should have someone ride home with him." Especially since Josh had to back out. Nate's younger brother had a mentor opportunity that combined theater and disabled children, and Nate had given his blessing. That was another change in him over the past four years.

"Just so you are aware." Nancy focused on Lauren. "Jet can be quite abrasive, and he likes to get things his way."

"True." Nate splayed his hands. "But I think this road trip would help him. And besides." He patted a fist over his heart. "It feels like God's telling me he should come."

How could she argue with one of Nate's God nudges? Every stray he'd picked up this past year had been the result of one of those proddings.

Still, apprehension stewed in Lauren's gut. Or was that her old foe, fear, invading again? Well, he wasn't allowed back in. She was no longer that frightened teen from five years ago. She'd learned how to stand up to her fear, rather than let it control her. This trip wouldn't be any different.

Lauren stood, taking control over the situation. "Let's go invite him."

Nate stood beside her and glanced at Nancy. "Do you know where he is?"

"Check the shop. He's taken a liking to working on cars." She picked up her glasses but didn't put them on. "A word of caution, Nate. Go into this road trip with your eyes wide open."

"We are." Lauren looked to Nate for confirmation.

He grinned. That word of caution was only an encouragement for him.

Nancy put on her glasses. "Remember, Nate, the same ground rules apply for Jet on the road as they do for Our Home. He messes up, it's tough-love time."

"Gotcha." Nate gave her a thumbs-up and turned to leave.

"One more thing, Nathan."

Nate groaned and turned back to Nancy. "What?"

She shook a finger at him. "No. More. Strays. Got that?"

"Yes, *Mom*." Nate smirked.

They finally escaped Nancy's office and hurried through the house that had once belonged to Nate's aunt and uncle, the same couple who'd created an apartment for Lauren in their Larchmont, New York home. The same couple who'd become like parents to her, even more so than Nate's folks.

She followed Nate through the kitchen and mudroom to what had once been a garage. Now it housed different training areas: woodworking, construction, art, and more. The young adults fortunate enough to find their home here would get much more than a roof over their heads. They learned many home basics like cooking, cleaning, home maintenance, self-maintenance, finances, things many people take for granted.

Some residents were studying for their GED, others were learning to fill out college applications. Plus, Bible studies were held once a week. Attendance wasn't mandatory, but highly recommended.

Best of all, Our Home was wrapped in prayer.

Of those who'd moved on, a vast majority had become successful, contributing members of society, rather than lurking on the outskirts, not sure where or how they fit in.

"There he is." Nate pointed to the far corner of the garage where denim-covered legs protruded from beneath the front of a car. A man squatted beside the legs, giving instructions. As she and Nate approached, the instructor patted those legs. "We've got company."

A man who looked inches taller than Nate—who was six-foot-two—slid from under the car. He wiped grease-stained hands on his jeans, and his near-black eyes cut her way, giving her the shivers.

Something about him was familiar, and that something wasn't good. Jet-black hair—was that where he got his name?—was tied back in a short ponytail. It took all her strength not to step back in fear. This was who Nate wanted to ride with them?

In her head, she recited the verse from 2 Timothy, "For the Spirit God gave us does not make us timid, but gives us power, love and self-discipline." With all the times she'd recited that verse to herself, one would think it would have taken root by now.

Regardless of where she may have seen him, he wouldn't be here if he wasn't eager to turn his life around. Masking her unease, she gave him a smile.

Which he didn't return. Okay then.

"Good to see you again." The volunteer trainer offered his hand to Nate.

"You too." Nate shook the man's hand. "Mind if I have a minute with Jet?"

"Sure thing. Be right back." The man slapped Jet on the back. "Good work there."

Finally, the slightest of smiles made an appearance followed by a hasty exit.

"Whatchya need?" Jet crossed his arms and leaned against the car, propping one ankle over the other.

"You know that road trip I'm going on?"

Jet shrugged. "What about it?"

"My little brother can't go, so I thought I'd invite you instead."

Finally, light flickered in Jet's eyes. "Seriously? You're asking me?"

"Thought you'd enjoy it."

Lauren elbowed Nate. "Introduce us?"

"Oh, uh, yeah. Jet, this is my sister, Lauren."

A grin broke through her fear. Nate had only recently dropped the "sort-of" from in front of "sister." Maybe they weren't blood siblings, but they were definitely siblings-at-heart.

"And Lauren, this is Jethro Wurm, AKA Jet, he's . . . "

Lauren heard nothing else as all her blood seemed to gush to her toes, and she became light-headed. She *had* seen Jet before. Years ago, during those awful middle school years she'd endured with no mother around to cry to.

Back then she'd known him as Jethro Wurm, the wormy bully who'd made those middle school years a living nightmare.

"Nice to meet you." Jet stuck out his hand, but slowly retracted it as Lauren's face turned an ashen white. She covered her mouth and mumbled something before she spun and made a hasty exit through the garage. What had he done wrong now?

Wait. Putting himself down for no reason—or any reason for that matter—was the exact type of thinking his counselor had warned him about. Casey would tell him to assess the situation before making any judgment. What were the facts?

A – Lauren is Nate's sister. Sort-of sister, that is. Nate had previously explained their complicated relationship.

B – Jet had only met Lauren this one time and knew little of her other than that she'd been taken in by Nate's family when her dad died.

C – All Jet had done in this exchange was to greet her and offer his hand. That was it.

Had he scowled, though? Getting rid of that constantly-angry face was one thing he had to work on. Still, a scowl usually didn't send people running away in fear.

Something jabbed his ribs and Jet shook himself back to the present.

"You okay?" Nate looked from Jet to the house entrance Lauren had retreated to. "You don't know each other, do you?"

Jet breathed in slowly then puffed it out to the count of four, a technique his counselor had taught him to deal with his mental beatings. "Never met her." Not that he remembered anyway. Was she someone he'd had to put on the street, courtesy of his mom's property management business? There'd been too many for him to remember each family and every stricken face as he'd evicted them from their apartments. Their homes.

Wouldn't they get a laugh out of him being the homeless one now?

"Huh. Weird." Nate shrugged. "I like Lauren, but she's always had this quirky side I don't get. You get used to it." He cocked a grin and rubbed his hands together. "Now back to our road trip. What do you think?"

Road-tripping with friends, with no one badgering him or putting him down. No one bossing him around, making him do their dirty work. Having fun for fun's sake. What would that be like? More than anything, he'd love to go, but there were obstacles.

"I'm supposed to be looking for a job." That was one of the conditions of him staying at Our Home.

"You can do that online, can't you? There'll be lots of time on the bus."

True. And if he did get interviews, he could set them up for when they returned. "When do you expect to be back?"

"Couple weeks." Nate bent over the engine of the Honda Accord Jet had been working on with the help of Gregg. The auto mechanic from Starr Repairs was one of the many volunteers at Our Home. Before coming here, Jet had no idea that people really wanted to help others. Especially someone like him.

"What's wrong with this car?" Nate went around to the driver's door.

Jet shrugged. "Nothing that I know of. Was just giving it an oil change." One of the many things Gregg had taught him since moving in a month ago. He pulled out the dipstick and wiped it on his work jeans. Then he stiffened, waiting for the reprimand for getting his pants dirty.

But none came. Would he ever get used to that? He returned the dipstick to the tube. "Why me?" Nate was one of those guys who always had friends around. Why wouldn't he ask one of them, someone he knew better?

Nate gestured to the car. "Reason number one. You're an engine whisperer. At least that's what Gregg tells everyone. Says you can make an old Cougar purr. I took The Draken in for a once-over, and they said it looks good, but stuff happens."

"I'm not that—" He stopped himself and struggled with spitting out his next words. "Th-thank you." His counselor had also encouraged him to think positively about himself and to accept compliments. Who knew that would be so difficult? Fact was, he was good with engines, and he enjoyed working on them, something he hadn't realized until he'd moved in here. Apparently, having a mechanical aptitude was a trait inherited from his dad, which meant his mom would hate him working on cars. But her opinion did not matter anymore. Gregg's did, and Nate's did.

"Reason number two." Nate made a motion like he had his hands on a steering wheel. "Josh had to cancel out, and Lauren doesn't like to drive big vehicles, and I'm gonna need a break on the road."

"Don't you need a commercial license to drive a bus?"

"Just your regular license."

"And you'd let me drive?"

"Of course. One thing my uncle drilled into me was that

distracted driving—and that means tired driving—isn't ever acceptable. He learned the hard way. I want to avoid the lesson."

And thanks to Nate, that was a lesson Jet hadn't had to learn the hard way. If Jet would have driven that night he'd literally bumped into Nate in the parking lot . . . He shivered just thinking about it.

But then, that night, he hadn't cared if he lived or not.

Things had changed. Nate credited God for the change. Everyone at Our Home seemed to credit God for things, yet they never pushed religion on him. Someday, he might even show up at the daily devotions.

"Reason number three." Nate pushed away from the Accord. "Josh and I had some fun stuff planned that Lauren's not into—"

"What kind of stuff?" Maybe he wasn't into that either.

"Baseball game in Milwaukee. Amusement park in Ohio. That kind of stuff."

Jet couldn't suppress a grin. "Sounds like my kind of fun." Things he hadn't taken time to do since his failed attempt at a college education. His mom's company had kept him too busy.

"And reason number four." Nate held up four fingers. "I like Lauren, but a week with only her? Might send me to the looney bin."

"Is she always that moody?" Jet thought back to her reaction when Nate introduced them. Had it somehow been his fault?

"Naw. When she moved in with the family, she was, but

her dad had recently died, so that was understandable. On top of that, I was a jerk to her. It's a miracle she even likes me."

"You? A jerk?" That wasn't at all who Jet had seen in Nate. From the moment Nate found him stumbling out of the bar toward his car until now, Nate had been nothing but a positive role model. As they were the same age, that meant something.

Nate snorted. "Just ask Josh. My parents. All my relatives. They'll give you an earful. Now Jaclyn, she's a little blind. She looks up to her big brother." Nate gestured toward the garage doors. "So, you coming with us or not?"

"On a few conditions."

"Name 'em."

"I help pay for gas."

"No argument there."

"And I pay my own way. Entertainment. Food. Lodging. Whatever."

"Oh, yeah, I forgot to mention that part of the deal." Nate grinned. "Lauren and I are broke, just-graduated-from-college people, so yeah, you pay your own way."

"Good. When do you leave?"

"There's the catch. We leave as soon as you can get ready. We've got tickets to the ballgame at Miller Park tonight and the drive is over six hours with food and bathroom breaks." He checked his watch. "How fast can you pack?"

"Five minutes." Considering he had only the few items he'd purchased since arriving at Our Home, packing wouldn't take long. "But, dude, you really want me to shower before we go."

Nate rubbed his nose. "Man, you're right. Take as much time in the shower as you need."

"Give me fifteen minutes."

"Sure that's enough?" Nate rubbed his nose again.

"Dude."

Nate laughed. "Fifteen minutes, and I'll meet you in Nancy's office. She wants to give us a send-off."

"I'll be there." And he couldn't be more excited either. For the first time in his life, things were looking up. Maybe he'd finally learn to leave the past where it belonged. Behind him.

What was wrong with her?

Lauren sat on the floor in the main floor bathroom, struggling to calm the shakes. She'd thought she'd exorcized those demons long ago, yet here she was trembling, afraid to step outside the door. How was she going to spend the next week in a cramped bus with him?

Did he remember her? Was she the only one, or had she been one in a succession of victims?

Every whispered name—Dummy, Klutz, Fatty—every subtle but hurtful action flitted through her brain like an old-time film. The milk "accidentally" spilling on her food. His foot "unintentionally" jutting out to trip her. The elbow "inadvertently" knocking her books from her hands. And so much more. No one had believed her that the angelic son of the city mayor was a bully.

No one but her dad. The school hadn't believed him either.

But that was years ago. Ten, to be exact. And she was no longer that scared, insecure little girl who had no clue how to defend or stand up for herself. What would Sheila tell her to do? Nearly five years ago, Nate's aunt had stepped into the mom role for Lauren, teaching her to overcome her insecurity. That was who Lauren needed right now.

Lauren got up and hugged her still-trembling body. One thing she'd been taught when dealing with bullies was to avoid them. No way could she avoid him on this road trip. She could always fly to New York instead. Yes, that was what she'd do. Now that Nate had a friend to join him, the two guys could travel across the country, stop at all the places Nate wanted to visit, and avoid those places Lauren had on her must-see list. It would be a win-win for all of them.

With a tissue, she wiped her eyes then reached for the doorknob. Someone knocked before she could turn it.

"You okay, Lauren?"

Nancy. Technically the administrator of Our Home, but emotionally a mom to so many who'd resided here.

Lauren cleared her throat. "Yes." Her voice wobbled. Naturally, Nancy had seen Lauren fly past the office to the restroom, and she'd be concerned. That was what made her so good in her job.

Putting on her best *I'm okay* face, she stepped out of the

bathroom.

Nancy's gaze probed Lauren's eyes that were probably veined in red. "Nathan said you were out in the shop and suddenly turned white as a ghost. Are you feeling well?"

Lauren shrugged, still not trusting her voice.

"Is it Jet? Do you know him?"

How did Nancy know that?

Nancy put her arm around Lauren's shoulders. "Want to talk about it?"

Yes, she did, but as much as Nancy was a mom to others, Lauren still relied on Sheila. Lauren sighed. "I need to talk with Sheila."

"Understood." Nancy squeezed Lauren's shoulders. "Go ahead and use my office. Take as long as you like."

"Thank you," Lauren whispered then slipped into the office and closed the door. She also drew the curtains on the French doors. Lauren had no doubt that her face would convey all her emotions when talking with Sheila.

She sat in Nancy's chair and spun to face the back wall made of bookshelves and a Murphy bed. A remnant from when Sheila and her husband Ricky lived here, before they established Our Home. She quick-dialed Sheila's cell. Normally, she didn't like bothering her at work, but this was an emergency. To Lauren anyway.

It rang four times before going to voice mail. Shoot! She left a brief message and reclined in Nancy's chair, her eyes closed. Now what? Nate wanted to leave right away, but if she stepped foot on that bus, she was certain that memories would flood through again. Riding with Jet would be torture. Well, she'd just have to tell Nate to head out without her. She'd use some of Sheila's frequent flyer miles to get her to New York early. That would give her time to . . .

Time to what? All her belongings were in the bus, so she wouldn't be able to set up her apartment. She squeezed her head between her hands. What was it Sheila would tell her to do if avoiding the bully wasn't possible?

Show confidence. Easier said than done. If Jet hadn't changed, she should stand up to him, tell him his behavior was wrong, and she wasn't going to put up with it. Again, easier said than done.

More than likely, Sheila would tell her to use this time as a learning opportunity.

The phone sang out "I Have Confidence" from *The Sound of Music.* Sheila's ringtone. Oh, to be like Maria from that movie! She steeled her voice before answering with a simple, "Hi."

"What's wrong, sweetie. You didn't sound good in your message."

She sighed. "Because I'm not," eked from her vocal cords.

"Talk to me."

Lauren stared at pictures on the bookshelves of the Our Home family, beginning with Sheila and Ricky and their son and daughter. A family meant to be photographed. They looked like they didn't have any problems. Lauren knew differently, and that was how she and Sheila connected so well.

"Remember me telling you about that boy back in

middle school? The one who bullied me until Dad had to pull me out?" He'd enrolled her in a different school, one that involved miles of traveling for him. But he'd sworn then his daughter was worth it.

"Of course. And you've run into him again."

Lauren laughed, but not with humor. "You could say that. He's Nate's latest project, and Nate just invited him on our bus ride."

Silence answered from Sheila's end. Lauren knew Sheila was contemplating the response. That was another lesson she'd taught Lauren. Listen and think before reacting. "What do you want to do?"

Another lesson she'd learned. Sheila never jumped in to solve Lauren's problems. Rather, she encouraged Lauren to think about what she could do herself to handle the issue.

"I want to fly to New York." In saying those words out loud, she knew what Sheila's answer would be, but hoped for a surprise.

"I see. Do you think that's the best way to deal with him? If you do, we'll fly you home."

No surprise. She also knew that if she chose flying, Sheila would be disappointed, and Lauren hated disappointing her.

Lauren sighed. "No. I should face him."

"That's my girl."

"But I really don't want to."

"Understandable, but you can do this, Lauren."

"I will." Although her insides still quaked and didn't match her promise to Sheila. Was that what facing her fears was all about?

They exchanged a few more words then said their goodbyes. Yes, Lauren would pull on her big girl panties and ride the bus with Jet. She'd just put on headphones and read a book in the back. It was one week with him. What could possibly go wrong?

Chapter Two

Showered and packed in less than fifteen minutes, Jet hurried outside with his plastic bag filled with clothes and toiletries. He stopped on the porch and gaped at Nate's tricked-out bus. "Man, this bus is sick!" A massive dragon's head was profiled on the side of the bus, otherwise painted in purple, and "The Draken" was painted beside it, in a font that reminded him of horns.

"Thanks, man." Nate joined him on the porch, carrying a forty-pack of bottled water, and a backpack slung over his shoulders.

"The Draken. Does that mean dragon?"

"Yep. I took the name from a Viking longship built a few years back, that sailed from Norway to the Great Lakes."

"Cool. Did you paint this?"

Nate shrugged. "Yep."

"You've got mad skills, man."

"Hope my new boss thinks so." He hefted the water. "This going to be enough for you?"

"Probably not." Jet grinned.

Nate headed for the bus. "I'm warning you, there's no toilet on The Draken."

"Guess we'll have to make pit stops."

"Guess so." Nate jutted his chin toward the water he carried. "Want this up front or in back?"

"Front." He'd probably go through those forty plus more on this road trip.

Nate tugged open the bus door.

"Clever." Jet examined the door that had once been a bi-fold. Now it opened like a regular house door and was even locked with a deadbolt.

"Thanks. Dad helped me rig it."

What would it be like to have a dad who helped with cool projects like this? What would it have been like to have a father who hadn't skipped out on his family ten years ago?

Not going there. Jet followed Nate onto the bus. Bad memories weren't allowed on this road trip.

The driver's seat looked like it was original, but nothing else inside was. A wood-like flooring was laid from the steps to a curtain midway to the back, and the walls were done in a reclaimed wood. Kitty-corner from the driver's seat was a captain's chair on a swivel and across from it was a dinette with bench seats on either side of a table.

"This is where you're sleeping." Nate carried the bottled water past the dinette and set it down on a bed made from four bus benches smooshed together. Definitely wouldn't be the most comfortable bed he'd slept on, but he'd make it work.

"And this is mine." Nate slung his bag on top of his bed—a real mattress propped up on a platform about four feet off the bus floor, right in front of the curtain.

Jet pulled the curtain aside. No bed for Lauren. Just a fridge a tad bigger than a dorm fridge, with cabinets above it, and a bunch of labeled boxes. Probably Lauren's stuff.

"Where does Lauren sleep?" Was there a bed behind her things so she'd have privacy?

Nate pointed to the dinette. "That folds to become a bed. One of the things I splurged on when renovating Draken. There's still things I want to do, but that'll come."

"I'm ready," a woman's voice said behind them.

He turned toward the front of the bus where Lauren stood. That sickly color had faded from her face, but now her unblinking eyes and the firm set of her mouth showed something new: anger.

Wasn't she too young to be one of his eviction victims? Hadn't she been living with Nate's family for the past few years?

Well, whatever made her upset with him, he was used to it. He felt bad for ruining her trip, but Nate needed him. He hoped he wouldn't ruin Nate's trip too.

His life experience told him that was no guarantee.

Lauren got off the bus and walked around to the back door, which Nate opened. She handed him her suitcase, and he squeezed it in amongst the boxes of her belongings, beside his duffel. Had Jet brought anything along? It wasn't uncommon for residents of Our Home to carry all their belongings in a trash bag, but she didn't even see one of those.

She glanced toward the house where Jet had gone to receive last-minute instructions from Nancy. How had the mayor's son come to live in a home for homeless young adults? From what Lauren remembered, the mayor had been wealthy, and the town had loved her.

So, what had happened?

Not that Lauren was going to find out. She planned to spend every moment she could away from him.

"Ready?" Nate closed the back door.

"I guess." She instantly regretted her lukewarm answer, so she glued on a smile and added. "I can't wait!" *Until I get to New York.*

"Uh-huh." Nate crossed his arms and stared down at her. "What's going on? Just yesterday you were all excited about the trip. Now today you're going old Lauren on me."

"Gee, thanks." *Old* Lauren never would have responded with sarcasm.

"Sorry, that was rude." Nate ran a hand through his short, curly blond hair. So many of her college friends had had crushes on him, it was nauseating. "But seriously. Your face turned so white when I introduced you to Jet, I thought you were going to faint. What's up with that?"

She looked down at the asphalt driveway and concentrated on the birds singing spring courting songs. "Nerves, I guess."

"Uh-huh. Like I believe that."

He'd become too intuitive of late, much like his mom.

But Nate didn't need to know about her past with Jet. Jet didn't either, for that matter. "Honestly, it's just nerves." And that was the truth, if only a part. "I've never gone on a trip like this before." That was true too. This was her first trip independent from older adults, and the idea had always scared her. It meant she really was an adult which brought a whole new set of responsibilities she wasn't certain she was prepared for.

Sheila had told her that her feelings and fears were normal, and with God by her side, she could face that fear. She'd be a fool if she let her memories of Jet ruin the trip for her, so once they got on the road, she'd spend time in the Word and praying.

"You guys ready?" Jet came around the back of the bus, a big grin on his face. He didn't look nearly as menacing as he had earlier either, wearing cargo shorts and a T-shirt with some *Star Wars* character on the front. His shoulder-length hair was now clean and free from its ponytail. Some women might call him cute.

But that was only on the outside.

She remembered the ugliness within.

And that sprouted something within her. Not the churning, I-need-to-get-away-from-him fear, but more of a bubbling I-want-to-get-in-his-face-and-tell-him-off feeling.

That wouldn't be right either, but it sure would feel good.

But acting out would ruin Nate's trip, so instead of following her gut, she forged a smile like the nice, polite Lauren would. "That's all I've got."

"Then let's get on board. I want to show Jet our plans

before we take off." With a grin the size of Lake Superior, Nate banged his fist on the side of The Draken. Then he walked to the front and opened the door for her.

The guys followed her past the driver's seat. Shoot, she'd forgotten that Jet would be riding in back with her. Since this was a school bus, there weren't two seats up front. Maybe he'd get lost in a book or in his phone. Wasn't that what guys did?

She sat at the dinette. Nate sat across from her, and Jet slid along beside her. Good. Then she wouldn't have to see his face.

Nate laid a sheaf of papers on the table. "I want Jet to know what to expect this week."

"Of course." She kept her tone neutral and her gaze on the paper.

Nate handed her and Jet an itinerary. "The trip is roughly thirteen hundred miles." He turned the page and pointed at a map. "The plan is to drive about four hundred miles a day, spending our nights at RV campgrounds."

"They have showers, I hope." Jet plugged his nose. "Six days on the bus with you and no shower doesn't sound like a picnic."

"The ones we're going to do." Nate laughed. "I learned the hard way from traveling with my brother." Nate pointed to Jet's itinerary where he had addresses, phone numbers, and websites written down. This was far too organized for Nate. His mom must have helped him. "Restrooms, showers, stores, swimming pools. We can grill on-site too, if we feel like cooking."

"So, we're roughing it." Jet grimaced.

He couldn't be serious, could he? That was what he called roughing it? Wasn't homeless living about as rough as you could get?

"Yep. Real rough." Nate grinned. "If we stick to this plan, it'll take us about four days of driving and give us a few days to play. We should arrive in New York six days from now."

"You mean we get to have fun, too?" Jet elbowed Lauren, and she nearly jumped from her bench seat.

The jab was innocent, but it still freaked her out. She edged away from him, gluing herself to the side of the bus covered in reclaimed barn wood from Nate's grandpa's farm.

"Maybe we can crash some parties along the way." Jet raised his hand as if holding a glass, and he tipped it toward his mouth. "You've got the bus to sleep it off in."

Nate stilled and gave Jet the same death glare she'd seen him give his younger brother. "Didn't you listen to anything Nancy had to say?"

"We're away from the house." Jet shrugged. "Who's it going to hurt?"

Nate grabbed the itineraries off the table and stabbed his finger toward the exit door. "If you're not going to take this seriously, you can leave right now. Our Home rules say *no alcohol*. On or off premises, if you want to stay there."

"Fine." Jet raised his hands in the air. "I was joking, okay?"

Sure didn't sound like he'd been joking.

"And no sleeping around either. I catch you with a girl,

and you're done."

"Dude, I said I was joking. You think I want to cross Nancy?"

"You'd better be joking," Nate mumbled under his breath.

What if Jet messed up on the way, broke Our Home rules? She stared out the window at the pine-surrounded driveway. What would happen to Jet then? Grrr. Why had Nate invited him in the first place?

"We're good then?" Amazing how much Nate sounded like his dad. Lauren certainly wouldn't cross him, and Jet better not either.

"Yeah. We're good. I'll behave."

Sheila would advise Lauren to give him a chance. Wasn't that what being a good Christian was about? Yet being around him resurrected all the feelings from her middle school years. Apparently, God had a lot of work to do in her yet. She prayed she'd be open to His molding.

"Okay." Nate cleared his throat and laid the papers back on the table.

Nate pointed to a campground by Milwaukee. "After tonight's game, we'll head here. Tomorrow . . . " His eyes lit up and he jutted his finger at a spot in Ohio by Lake Erie. "We head to Cedar Point."

"Sweet!"

Good. Jet was as excited about rides as Nate. Maybe that meant she could get out of doing the amusement park thing. Roller coasters scared the life out of her. She'd told Nate she'd go so he wouldn't be alone, but now that wasn't a problem. With Jet along, she'd get to stay in the bus and read.

Wait. Wasn't the amusement park expensive? Where would Jet come up with the money? She and Nate had just graduated college and certainly didn't have extra. "You know, Nate. Cedar Point isn't exactly cheap."

"Yeah, so? I thought you said you could afford it."

"I can, but . . . " She tried to nod discreetly toward Jet.

"How about I spring for it as a thank-you for bringing me along."

Say what? Lauren jerked her head toward Jet. The guy must be clueless. "I'm fine, my question is whether you can afford it."

"Money's not an issue," Jet said nonchalantly with a serious face and no hint of irony.

"He's right, Lauren."

She stared at Nate, who nodded and didn't offer any further explanation. Okay, Jet having money made no sense. Homeless people did not have money to spend on amusement parks or baseball games or road-tripping across the country.

"Fine." She raised her hands in the air. One plus one didn't equal two here, but Nate wasn't worrying, so why should she? As long as she and her belongings—most of them mementoes of her mom and dad—arrived in New York in one piece, she was good.

Nate cleared his throat and pointed again at the itinerary. "We'll stay three nights in Sandusky, then head to Hershey, Pennsylvania."

"Hershey?" Jet sounded like a little child anticipating going to the fair for the first time.

"Yep, home of Hershey Park, another great amusement park that Lauren already vetoed."

"Sure, make me the bad guy." Lauren teased back.

"Well, it's true." Nate pretended to pout. "I gave you a baseball game and two days at Cedar Point. You gave me a few hours at Hershey Gardens. If you guys don't complain about that, then we can go on a chocolate tour."

"If I have to." Nate sighed and grinned at Jet. "I hear they give you chocolate samples all over town."

"I'm not much for chocolate." Jet shrugged. "But I've always wanted to go to Hershey."

Seriously? He didn't like chocolate, but wanted to go to Hershey? And he wasn't even bothered that they weren't going to Hershey Park. Things still didn't add up.

And why wasn't Nate bothered?

He continued on with the itinerary. "From Hershey, it's only a couple hundred miles to Larchmont, Lauren's new home." He stacked his papers together. "Now if everything goes right on the way out, there's no saying we can't stop at Hershey Park or Six Flags on the way home."

Now that was a smart idea.

"Sounds good to me." Jet folded his hands and tucked them behind his head. "I'm just along for the ride."

"It's a plan." Nate got up and pulled keys from his pocket. "Then I say it's time we took off. Buckle up, we're heading to Milwaukee."

Jet sprawled out on the bus cushions that would be his bed for the next several nights. He felt like Bilbo going off on an adventure to the unknown. No, he wasn't roughing it like Bilbo Baggins had in *The Hobbit*, but compared to what Jet was used to, this was practically a cardboard box.

He'd never felt so free.

"Just entered cheesehead territory," Nate called from the front of the bus.

Wisconsin. The place where his father had first run off to years ago. Not with his secretary. No, that would have been too cliché. He'd run off with Mother's secretary instead. That day she'd lost two people she should have been able to trust.

Mother didn't realize it, but that day Jet had also lost the two people he should trust: both his father and his mother.

But Jet had done his research over the years. His dad had moved on from Wisconsin. Whether the secretary had moved with him, Jet didn't know.

What he did know was that his dad never paid a cent of child support. Jet's mom had screeched that often enough to have it forever tattooed on his brain.

So far at Our Home, no one had let him down. No one had accused him of doing something he hadn't done. No one called him names. He'd be a fool if he sought out a party on this trip. For the first time in his life, he didn't feel like he needed to escape from reality.

Besides, his reality at the moment was a tricked-out school bus. Nate had told Jet he still had plans for The Draken, when he got the money.

If Nate let him, Jet would be glad to pitch in. It sure would be nice to lay claim to doing something positive, something tangible, visible, with his hands. Maybe then, Mother would be proud of him.

He lay back on the seat, tucked his hands beneath his head, and closed his eyes.

Seemed he'd barely shut them when the bus jerked, and rumble bumps vibrated beneath him. He sat up and grabbed the windowsill to keep from falling onto the floor as the bus jerked to the right.

Lauren screamed.

And Jet flung out a curse word as The Draken careened off the road.

Chapter Three

*L*auren gasped, and her Kindle went flying. The bus swerved off the highway. She grasped the table in front of her, wishing for seatbelts. The Draken was doing a tight tango with the ditch and blacktop. Ahead, a bridge guardrail seemed to race toward the bus. Her breaths came in quick waves. Lauren closed her eyes and prayed but couldn't block out squealing brakes and the crunch of gravel.

And then there was silence, but for the heavy breaths of the bus's occupants.

Then an angry curse word hurled from Jet's mouth. "You trying to kill us, man?"

Nate didn't answer. Rather, he glared at Jet from the mirror above the driver's seat.

"Wh . . . what happened?" Lauren managed to eke out, her heart rate slowing, but far from normal.

"Deer." Nate grumbled and unbuckled himself. After flipping the hazard-light switch, he hurried down the stairs and off the bus. Jet was right on his tail, followed by Lauren.

She glanced ahead at the bridge looming just feet ahead

of them and the steep ravine it crossed and gulped. They'd stopped just in time.

But Nate didn't seem concerned about that. He stared westward, the direction they'd come from, and Jet and Lauren did the same.

She saw nothing but a steady stream of cars, trucks, and semis which all blew past, too busy to stop and help. "Did you hit one? Is Draken okay?"

"Clipped one. Came out from the trees . . . " Nate shook his head, his chest rapidly rising and falling with fear-born breath. "Must have kept running. I'd already counted ten deer in the ditch, and was watching, but he came out so fast."

"It's not your fault, Nate." Lauren laid a hand on his shoulder.

He shook it off. "I was driving."

"And deer come out of nowhere. That's what they do. My dad had two pickups totaled by deer." She surveyed both sides of the road. Not an animal to be seen. Now.

Nate trudged to the front of the bus. There, he knelt by the front bumper and uttered something under his breath.

Jet squatted beside him. "Sorry, man. I didn't mean to jump on you."

Nate rubbed his hand over a deep indentation in the bumper's metal, pushing it nearly into the front tire. "It's okay. We all were excited. Never hit a deer before."

"Me neither. And I was asleep for this one." He gestured toward the bruised bumper. "Can I take a look?"

"Be my guest."

Jet laid down on the gravel and scooted beneath the front end of the bus. He pushed on the bumper, moving it away from the tire, but not completely straightening it. Then he slid out from beneath the bus and wiped off his backside. "Could have been worse. Just a little body damage. Tires look good. Engine looks unaffected. Give me some time at a campground, and I'll whip it back into shape." He touched the headlight closest to the damaged bumper. "Want to give the lights a try?"

The hazard lights were blinking. Hopefully, that meant the other lights worked too.

"Good idea." Nate hopped onto the bus. The left headlight came on, but not the right.

Jet gave Nate a thumbs-down signal, and Nate slumped from the bus.

"I take it you don't have an extra?"

"That's about the only thing I don't have." Nate shook his head.

"Then we'll get one at the next town." Jet wiped his hands together. "Doesn't look too hard to fix."

"Hope you're right." Nate gestured to the bus. "Let's head out before stores close. I don't want to be driving around Milwaukee with a broken headlamp."

They all scrambled onto the bus, and Jet volunteered to take over driving responsibilities. That was perfectly fine with Lauren. Then she didn't need to work at avoiding him.

She found her Kindle jammed against the driver's seat and claimed her spot at the dinette.

"Need a drink?" Nate hollered from the back. "A

munchie?"

"No thanks." After the excitement, Lauren had no appetite.

"Just bring me a bottled water." Jet started up Draken, and it seemed to purr just as nicely as it had before the deer decided to play chicken.

After bringing a bottle of water to Jet, Nate sat across from Lauren with enough chocolate and chips to last the week.

"Sure you have enough there?" She giggled, hoping to ease some of his stress.

He scratched his head. "Should hold me 'til supper."

The guy probably wasn't kidding.

"By the way, you did a good job handling Draken back there. I had visions of us lying upside down in the ditch."

"Or flipping over the bridge rail." Nate's hands shook as he tried opening a bag of chips.

She took the bag and opened it for him. "But we didn't, and that's to your credit."

"Appreciate it." He emptied the bag of chips and downed a candy bar before she'd even read a page. "I'm gonna go make a phone call."

The rest of the ride to Miller Park, where the Minnesota pro baseball team was due to play against Milwaukee, was uneventful. With the help of an auto store clerk, Jet had installed the new headlamp in minutes. She prayed the run-in with the deer was the last of their excitement on this trip.

Jet felt like running across the parking lot toward the stadium. He'd never been to a ballgame away from home before. His mother would have decried it as a waste of time. Anything fun had been a waste in her eyes.

But going to ballgames was something he'd always wanted to do with his father. He hadn't given up on that hope of going to a ballgame or doing other father-son stuff together.

He was quickly learning that just because his mother said something, didn't mean that was the truth. Just because she never missed an opportunity to call him an idiot, didn't mean he was dumb.

Which he wasn't.

His mother had always complained that his father was a wealthy deadbeat who cared about nobody but himself. Was that a lie as well?

But why would he have abandoned Jet if what his mother said wasn't true?

Don't go there, Jet. Don't see trouble where there isn't any.

Musing about his parents had slowed him down, so he began jogging toward the entrance. With security being so tight nowadays, lines reached halfway to the parking lot. He skipped past the first couple lines, then saw an opening in the middle of the third where people weren't paying attention. He should be able to sneak in without a problem. He jogged toward the opening, waving at Nate and Lauren to hurry.

"What are you doing?" Nate hissed when he caught up, then he gestured toward the end of the line where Lauren already stood. His friend was way too goodie-two-shoes at times. "We don't butt in."

"Yeah, buddie." A Milwaukee-shirt-wearing fan gave Jet a shove. "No butting in line."

"Watch it." Jet's hand balled into a fist and he held it inches from the fan's face.

"Jet!" Nate grabbed his arm and tried to yank it away.

He glared at his friend, intending to spew a few words he knew Nate would freak out over, but Nate wore his I-mean-business face, accompanied with crossed arms, and Jet knew he'd gone too far. Again.

When would he learn?

He lowered his hand and arm and offered a mumbled "Sorry," to the Milwaukee fan, then kept his head down as he followed Nate to where Lauren waited, her eyes throwing darts his way.

"What was that about?" Anger simmered in Lauren's hushed voice.

"I . . . " Jet stared outward toward the parking lot. He had no excuse other than that his temper always got the best of him. Even after working with his counselor, Casey, for the past month, he'd gained little control over that demon. "I'm sorry." He glanced from Lauren to Nate.

"Yeah, well . . . " Nate stepped forward in line, his

shoulders rigid as a two-by-four. "No more mess-ups, got it?"

"Yeah." Got it. He'd thought he could easily go a couple weeks without his idiot-self taking over, especially around Nate, but he hadn't even lasted a day. His mother was right. He was defective. If he was a praying man like Nate, this would be a good time to ask for help.

"Then I forgive you." Nate gave him a playful shove. "Let's go enjoy the game."

"You're good?" People didn't really forgive that quickly, did they?

"You said you're sorry. I forgave you. Period."

"Thanks, man." Made him want to try even harder at taming his temper. He could do it.

After waiting in line for a shorter amount of time than Jet expected, Nate led them through security. They found their seats without any more incidents, not that he hadn't wanted to react a couple of times. But he hadn't reacted. That was good, right?

As an additional apology, and hoping to smooth things over with Lauren too, Jet purchased four hot dogs, fries, and a drink for them and a turkey wrap for himself.

He handed a tray of food to Lauren, who'd insisted that Nate sit between them.

She accepted the food with a muttered, "Thank You."

What was up with her? He gnawed on his wrap while watching her out of the corners of his eyes. Nate had forgiven him and moved on, but she hadn't said two words to him since his episode outside the stadium. She hadn't looked at him or acknowledged him in any way, and it made him want to sink into the concrete. She had to know him from somewhere.

Hopefully, before their trip ended, he'd find out where they'd connected, and he'd make amends like his counselor had recommended. If he never learned what he'd done wrong, these six days on the bus could be a real long trip.

The bus pulled into the campground, and Lauren ran to the restroom while Jet and Nate checked in.

Coming out of the stall, she caught a glimpse of herself in the mirror and barely recognized herself. Gone was the shy, eye-downcast girl. Rather, she'd come face-to-face with someone who had pinched lips and unforgiving eyes.

She'd been a jerk to Jet. Still was, for that matter.

Yeah, Jet had been in the wrong, but as the Christian, wasn't she supposed to forgive him? Maybe so, but every time she looked at him, anger roiled inside her, and she'd avoided opening her mouth for fear of that anger spilling out.

By the looks of her reflection, anger had spilled out anyway.

She washed her hands, while asking God to wash her clean again. That seemed to be a daily prayer. Then she asked for words to say to Jet.

The simple answer came: *Will you forgive me?*

She dried her hands beneath the loud dryer, but still heard someone yelling, calling another person names she couldn't repeat.

Jet.

That too-familiar dread clawed up her throat as she entered the lobby area, confirming that Jet was doing the name calling, while flailing his arms in the air.

Nate paced across the lobby but wasn't doing anything to calm Jet or remove him from the situation.

She approached him and whispered, "What's going on?"

He ran a hand through his hair. "They lost our reservation. Said there's nothing else available. I can't get Jet to shut up. He's gonna get us kicked out of here and then The Draken will be dirt across the U.S. Can you talk him down?"

Her? What if he took his rage out on her instead?

Chapter Four

"**M**e?" Wincing at Jet's ongoing rant, Lauren pressed a hand to her chest and felt her heart pounding. "What can I possibly say?"

"I don't know." Nate shook his head then looked straight into her eyes. "Can you try?"

How could she say no, even though she was terrified? "I'll see what I can do. In the meantime . . . " She pointed to his phone. "You start looking for alternative campsites."

She shook her arms, trying to chase the jitters as she approached Jet. Not wanting to startle him, she came up beside him at the counter and said as calmly as her nervous voice could, "Jet."

His face was firetruck red when he turned to her. "What?" he growled.

And she couldn't help but retreat a step. Just like she always had back in middle school. But that girl had grown up and wouldn't be bullied. Lauren swallowed the massive lump building in her throat, looked Jet in the eye, and gestured to Nate. "He's finding something else." She said with a calm and confidence that didn't match her insides. "We're good."

"So?" He jabbed a finger at the young woman manning the counter, who was near tears. "They messed up. They need to make it right."

She dared to take his arm and pull it back. "Yeah, they messed up. It happens. Just like I've messed up. And Nate?" She forced a smile. "He's the king of messing up." She was certain payback would be coming from Nate for that statement.

But it seemed to register with Jet. The red slowly faded from his face, and he sagged against the counter, his breath coming out in swift waves. "Go ahead and say it. I screwed up again."

"Yeah, you did."

He drew a hand down his face. "I don't know what comes over me."

"You had a long, stressful day." Not that that was an excuse for taking it out on the poor girl behind the counter. Once a bully, always a bully.

And yet, he was still a child of God.

With that reminder, Lauren latched onto his arm and pulled him away from the counter. He didn't resist.

Nate held up his phone. "I found us a place."

She looked upward and whispered, "Thanks." Now to apologize to the employee, without making excuses for Jet. Back when he'd bullied her in middle school, the rare times people noticed, they always made excuses for him. She would not.

Again, she looked upward seeking help. No way could she do this on her own. Only then did she approach the clerk. "I am so sorry for that, and I have no excuse for his behavior. Is there anything I can do to make it up to you?"

The girl wiped her nose. "Just get him out of here."

"Right away." She turned and ran smack into a wall— make that Jet.

His face scrunched up. "Sorry." And he stepped past her.

With hands deep in his pockets, he stopped at the front counter. "I . . . I'm sorry."

Lauren stared at his back. He apologized?

"Did Jet just do what I think he did?" Nate came up beside her.

All she could do was nod.

"I, um." Jet sighed. "I'm working on anger issues, and I've obviously got a long way to go. I hope you can forgive me, but I understand if you don't."

Whoa. Those words came out of Jethro the Wormy Bully?

The clerk muttered something Lauren couldn't understand, then Jet trudged back to Lauren and Nate.

"Let's go." He strode past them, and they followed him to the bus. He stopped at the door and looked back at them. "Look. I know I blew it again, but that's what my mother does. When she gets in people's faces, they move the earth for her." He looked toward the building. "I make people cower."

"Yes." Lauren touched his arm. "But then you did the right thing. You apologized."

"If you guys want to send me home, I understand. That's twice in one day. You don't want me messing up your whole trip." He pulled out his phone. "If you drop me off at an airport, I'll fly home."

"Put that thing away." Nate pointed to the phone. "You're not getting out of this trip that easily. We need you, and you obviously need us. You learned a lesson back there. If you repeat it, yeah, you can go home. Three strikes and you're out. But I have faith that won't happen again."

"I'm with Nate." Had those words just passed her lips? Here, Jet was offering to go home, which would take a whole bunch of stress off her, and she was encouraging him to stay?

"Besides, when we go to Cedar Point, I need someone to ride the coasters with me." Nate gestured with his thumb toward Lauren. "Chicken here won't go on them."

She crossed her arms and stood tall. "No I won't. Nate needs you."

"You guys sure?"

"Get on the bus, man. I'm tired. I want to find the campground."

"Yes, sir." And with a smile, Jet opened the bus door.

Hopefully, tomorrow the only adventure they'd have would be on the rides.

Jet leaped up from his bed the moment the bus was parked at a different campground. He'd called his counselor the second he got on the bus, and Casey had encouraged Jet to call again when they arrived at a place where he could be alone. All Jet knew was that he was no better than his mother when it came to temper. Difference was, she knew how to use her anger to gain what she wanted.

And him? He just erupted. Then instead of feeling better about taking the situation into his own hands, instead of feeling like he was in command, he felt lousy and completely out of control.

The anger that had boiled over at the other campground, still seethed inside him, even though they'd been on the road for half an hour. He couldn't think of one tool Casey, his counselor, had given him for dealing with that anger, so he hurried from the bus with a quick, "I need to go for a walk." Thankfully, they didn't stop him or nose into his business. They just let him go. They probably were happy he left.

He found a path that led through a patch of woods and down to an empty beach. During the day this place was likely buzzing with families playing together.

What would that have been like?

No. Don't go there. Leave the past in the past.

Instead, he closed his eyes and focused on the night sounds: a gentle lapping of water, a choir of crickets, leaves dancing in the breeze. If only he could carry this place in his back pocket. He sat near the water, pulled off his shoes, and soaked his feet in the frigid lake. Didn't bother him, but rather it relaxed muscles that were too tense from his anger eruption, and it helped him focus.

Find a quiet place was one of the most helpful tools

Casey had given him for dealing with his anger. Casey's advice must be helping. Jet had pulled out this *Quiet Place* tool without realizing that was what he'd done.

His emotions finally in check, he sat down on the sandy beach and dialed Casey. He confessed what he'd done not more than an hour earlier and his reaction at the baseball game, and how he felt about those events now.

Then he tensed for the verbal whipping.

Which never came.

Of course it hadn't, but the anticipation was always there. Casey called it a learned reaction.

Casey never condemned him, no matter how lousy Jet had acted. Instead, he always had a tool ready to give Jet so that an incident wouldn't be repeated. Tonight was no exception.

"Let's figure out what we need to pull from your anger management toolkit."

Jet mentally pictured a red toolkit, the imaginary one he stored all Casey's helpful tools in.

"Now take out your RAIC."

Jet grinned. "Dude, I don't keep the RAIC in the toolkit. I hang it on the garage wall."

And Casey laughed. Humor. Another tool Casey had given him.

"Good one, Jet." He cleared his throat. "Now you've got the RAIC. What do you do with it?"

Jet closed his eyes and pictured a four-pronged rake with the letters RAIC spelled across the prongs. The words *Listen * Think * React* were burned into the rake's handle.

He'd skipped right over listening and thinking. "First I *Recognize Warning Signs.*" Feeling tense. Breathing hard. Clenched fists. Tight jaw and shoulders.

"Were they there?"

"Every single one of them."

"And what did you do with that recognition."

He sure didn't *Assess the Situation* like he was supposed to. "I didn't assess, I just reacted."

"Good. You recognize that. That's a step forward."

Sure felt like a step backward to him. Jet picked up a stone the size of a softball and hurled it toward the water. It landed with a loud splash.

Like his anger. Made a big splash but accomplished nothing but sinking him to the bottom. Before Casey could ask him about the letter I, Jet blurted out, "I didn't *Identify My Trigger*, which in this case, was someone messing up my plans. I wasn't in control." In more ways than one. Getting in someone's face worked well for his mom, which was where he'd learned the reaction, but it only made people fearful of him.

But his mom wasn't to blame for his actions. Not anymore. *Taking Responsibility for Your Actions* was one of the first tools Casey had given him. And when he blamed his mother, he was giving her too much control.

"See, you're learning, Jet."

"It sure doesn't feel like it."

"After an incident, it's not going to feel right. The key is to take this incident and ask yourself what you can learn from it, and you have been learning. You've already applied the fourth prong here."

Jet pictured the rake with the words *Cool Down* etched on the final prong. "I found a quiet place and called you." Cooling down had taken him too long, but coming here to the water's edge had soothed his temper. If only he could keep a lake in his back pocket.

"You are learning."

Jet sighed. "I'm trying."

"You're succeeding, Jet. Remember that. Absorb that."

"Okay. I'm working on it." And he had changed, even though Nate and Lauren probably believed differently. His thoughts went back to the last time he'd seen his mother.

Someone had keyed the hood on her new Cadillac, and she drove to his apartment and pounded on his door. Pretending he wasn't home hadn't worked. She had a key, which was no surprise as his place was owned by his mom's company, TC Property Development. Feigning sleep hadn't worked either. Acting like he didn't care only provoked her more. And all his denials, which were the truth, fell on deaf ears.

His solution? Shove past her, take his keys and give her a real reason to be angry at him. The curse word he'd carved on her hood was what finally cost him his job at his mother's business and got him kicked out of his apartment. And then sent him on an alcohol binge.

Which was where he'd run into Nate. Literally.

His mother's anger hadn't ever fixed what was wrong either. Her yelling only made him feel worthless. Which was probably how he'd made that clerk back at the other campground feel.

All he'd accomplished by letting anger take control was scaring the dickens out of some minimum wage worker for something she likely wasn't responsible for. Just like him and his mom's car. He'd managed to get Nate angry with him. Nate, who had already sacrificed so much for their friendship. No wonder the only friends Jet had were the ones he bought drinks for at the local bar. And Lauren? She was frightened of him already. That vibe came through loud and clear. Yet tonight she'd calmed him.

He vowed to do better from now on.

"How are you feeling now?" Casey interrupted Jet's musing.

"Sort of depressed that I dumped on my friends like that. I volunteered to go home."

"Interesting."

Jet rolled his eyes. He hated it when Casey said that. What did *interesting* mean anyway?

"How did they react to your offer?"

"They talked me into staying." With unbelievable grace. Maybe that song "Amazing Grace" came from a similar situation.

"Sounds like you've surrounded yourself with good friends. They might be the most important tool you have."

Jet agreed a hundred percent.

"Jet, you out here?" Nate's voice came from behind him.

"I'm by the lake," he yelled back, then spoke into his phone. "Speaking of friends, I should go. Thanks for the talk."

"I'm always here for you."

And that had been the truth. Not once had Casey let him down, though Jet was certain he'd let Casey down in a hundred different ways. He hit End Call as Nate emerged from the tree line.

"You okay, man?" Nate kept his distance.

"I am now." He held up his phone and pocketed it. "Talked with Casey. We polished up some tools."

"Mind if I borrow a tool or two sometime?"

Jet laughed. "Doubt you'll need these."

"Ha. Ask Lauren about that. To be honest, I've got my own toolbox full of helps. Even with good parents, I tried pulling some junk on them. It's a miracle I made it out of my teens." Nate joined him by the water. "Why don't you come back now? Lauren's sleeping already, and I've got our beds made. If sleep wasn't one of the tools Casey gave you, it should have been."

"Dude, that was the first one he gave me."

"Then let's put it to some good use."

Chapter Five

The next morning, Jet sat up and stretched the kinks out in his back. Sleep hadn't come easily last night. It might be the most important item in is toolkit, but it was also something he couldn't seem to control. Trying to sleep on the former bus benches didn't help either.

He heard movement behind him and turned as Nate hopped down from his bunk.

Jet flung his legs over the side of his bed. "Sleep well?"

"Like a baby. You?"

"I'm thinking we need to stop somewhere and pick up an inflatable mattress."

"Not a bad idea. We could have a piece of MDF cut the exact size to lay over the benches, then put the mattress on there."

"Now you're thinking."

"And that's on a full bladder and an empty stomach." Nate hurried past him and Lauren who appeared to be sleeping yet.

Jet studied Lauren's face, peaceful in sleep. Round cheeks with a smattering of freckles framed by reddish-brown hair usually kept in a ponytail. Cute even. If she wasn't so freaked out by him, she'd be cuter yet.

He scratched his head. There was nothing familiar about her, at all. But he'd hurt so many people over the years, he couldn't remember every face. Would she warm up to him today? Not if he didn't keep his temper in check. He had to remember his tools.

All three travelers took quick showers, had some breakfast, then Jet took the driver's seat and headed south. Sandusky, Ohio, home to Cedar Point, one of the wildest amusement parks in the world, was about four hundred miles away. With bathroom and food breaks, they planned to be on the road about seven and half hours. Chicago was under two hours away, so Jet would drive through the city on I-90, then they'd switch drivers after that.

The fact that Nate trusted him with The Draken on city highways meant a lot. Mother never would have surrendered the reins to her favorite vehicle, and if she had, she would have been the worst backseat driver ever.

Nate never said a word.

"Hey, Jet, did you see that sign?"

Okay, he rarely said a word. "What sign?"

Nate took the captain's chair, kitty-corner behind Jet. "It said something about Jelly Belly factory tours. I heard they give free samples."

"Seriously?" Lauren chimed in, excitement in her voice.

A few years back, Jet would have loved the idea, but things had changed. He shot a quick glance to Nate. "You know, if we want to make it through Chicago before rush hour, we should keep moving." He refocused on the road.

"You're probably right." Lauren sighed.

Lauren agreed with him? Huh. Maybe he was making headway with her.

Or maybe he was reading too much into a few little words.

"Fine." Nate sighed loudly. "But I was really tasting those ear wax jelly beans." Nate slapped Jet on the back then joined Lauren at the dinette.

"Gross." He heard a shiver in Lauren's voice. "What are you, five?"

"Man, I'm with Lauren." Jet looked in the mirror above the windshield. "You seriously want to try ear wax jelly beans?"

"You don't?"

"Never been a goal." But having fun with friends who trusted and respected him? Friends who laughed with him? That had been a lifelong goal he hadn't thought was possible.

Not until now anyway.

In a little over an hour, they were passing through the outskirts of Chicago. Minneapolis traffic had nothing on this city's congestion. They were going all of ten miles an hour on the freeway. At this rate, they may as well add another couple hours to their trip.

To pass time, he chose his Road Tripping playlist on his phone, and the music played over the speakers Nate had rigged on the bus. He started jamming to a song. Lauren joined in, and then Nate did too, but Jet wouldn't classify what Nate was doing as singing.

"Dude!" Jet glanced in the mirror above the steering wheel and watched Nate dance in the aisle. "Listening to you sing is almost as bad as eating ear wax jelly beans."

Nate stilled and splayed a hand over his heart. "If I didn't know I sang like a warped record album, I'd be offended."

"Ha!" Lauren laughed. "Don't insult the record album."

Nate feigned a punch in her direction. She raised both fists and pretended back.

What would it have been like to grow up with siblings to laugh and fight with?

Apparently, he had some, if his research on his father was correct. Maybe he'd meet them soon and get to be a big brother.

Or maybe that was another worthless dream.

Nope. No negativity on this drive. He turned up the volume and let the music take him to another place.

Wait. Was that smoke?

Oh my gosh, yes! Pluming out from beneath the engine hood! He needed to get off the freeway now.

"Nate." He hollered to get his attention. "We've got a problem. Help me watch for exits."

Nate groaned and hurried to the captain's chair. "There." Nate pointed up ahead. "About a mile up on your right."

If they made it that far. First, he had to cross three lanes of bumper-to-bumper traffic.

That familiar tension squeezed his muscles and accelerated his heartbeat as he glanced at each mirror and saw lanes of vehicles crawling along on the freeway, leaving no room for a toy car, much less a bus. What if they stalled right here?

His fingers white-knuckled on the steering wheel. No! He was not going to give in to his anger.

While inhaling a deep breath, he flicked on his right blinker and hoped drivers would make space. Ha! They only tightened their grip on the bumpers in front of them.

He turned the steering wheel slightly to the right, as if moving into the adjacent lane regardless of the cars beside him, and finally a little Saturn slowed, giving Jet just enough room to squeeze in The Draken.

Whew. Only two lanes to go, and three-quarters of a mile to get there.

With the back of his hand, he wiped perspiration from his forehead. Smoke continued to curl from beneath the hood.

"He's making room!" Nate hollered.

Jet checked his side mirror and watched a vehicle peel back, with the driver gesturing for him to move over. Jet fitted the bus into the space and gave a Thank-You wave to the driver.

One lane to go.

A half mile to the exit. And a whole bunch of vehicles wanting to become part of a car-accordion. He nudged his steering wheel to the right, and someone laid on their horn. Another driver gave Jet a one-fingered salute, that Jet really wanted to return.

The exit loomed closer. If they couldn't get off, they might be stuck on the side of the freeway.

Finally, a car with Minnesota license plates made room

for him. Jet started into the lane, but the vehicle behind him—a Smart car—pulled into the open space. Jet bit back a nasty name. The Draken could crush that so-called car with one swipe.

The tiny car puttered past, and the Minnesota vehicle once again held back, creating a just-big-enough opening.

"You're good!" Nate yelled as Jet swerved into the right lane and immediately onto the exit. He veered onto the curb and then onto the edge of a grassy embankment, getting as far over as he could.

This wasn't his fault, he knew that in his head, but his heart could see his mom jabbing a finger his way, telling him anything he touched turned to dust.

Holding her breath, Lauren stared straight ahead as Jet calmly moved The Draken across three lanes of busy traffic and onto an exit ramp where he parked.

Nate hustled past her, and she followed him once the bus came to a complete stop. Jet zoomed out the door and lifted the hood. Smoke rose from the engine, yet the guys just stood there, staring at it.

Hoping to get far away in case of an explosion, she jogged up the grassy embankment and then looked back. The guys remained gawking at the engine. Were they idiots or what? She cuffed her hands around her mouth and yelled to them. "Nate, Jet, get away from there."

They both looked back at her with puzzled expressions.

Did they have a death wish, or what? Well, she'd get them away if she had to drag them. She hurried to them and tugged on their arms. "Come away! It could explode!"

They laughed—laughed!—at her.

Nate finally stepped back and took her arm, leading her away from the bus. "It's not gonna blow. That's steam. The engine's just overheating."

Just? She looked around trying to get a grasp of where they were. In the middle of a tangle of roads, that was where. "Okay . . . What does that mean? Are we stuck here . . . ?"

"We are stuck for a bit." Jet joined them, wiping his hands on what had been clean jeans. "Once the engine's cool, we'll check the radiator fluid, make sure that's full. If it's full, the radiator cap might be the problem. A cheap fix. Or it could be a bad thermostat. Another easy fix. Or a hole in a hose."

"There's a 'but' coming, isn't there?" Nate stuck his hands in his pockets and focused on his bus.

"'Fraid so. It could be your cooling fans or radiator or head gasket . . . You really don't want it to be the head gasket. Problem is, we won't know anything until the engine's cool."

"Wonderful." Nate kicked at the roadside gravel then plopped down on the edge of the incline. He held his head in his hands and mumbled an apology to Lauren.

"Not your fault." She sat beside him and circled her arms around her knees. "What do you want to do now?"

"I'm checking." Jet joined them on the ground, his focus

on his phone. After a few minutes, he set the phone aside. "I'd recommend waiting fifteen, twenty minutes, then I can check it out."

"Fine." Nate growled. He got up, wiped the grass from his behind, and returned to the bus.

She'd give him a few minutes alone before trying to give some vapid words of comfort. But that also meant staying outside here with Jet. Not a good option. She got up and aimed for the bus.

"It's probably best to give him some space," Jet said behind her.

She didn't like it, but Jet was right, so she sat near him again. Now what? Ignore him like she really wanted to do or be polite as her father had taught her.

She tugged on a piece of grass and choked out the words, "How long have you been working on cars?"

He looked at her like she'd grown horns. "She speaks."

So he had noticed her avoidance of him. She stared across the bustling freeway.

"Yeah, sorry about that." She blew out a breath. "I'm not terribly good with people." Which was true, but only part of the truth.

He laughed, the kind filled with irony rather than humor. "You and me both. Nate's the first guy I could really call 'friend' since . . . since I can't remember."

"You couldn't have a better friend than Nate."

"Agreed. No one else cared. Guys just hung out with me for . . . "

For what? She wouldn't ask him yet. She hadn't earned the right to go deeper with him. One thing she already knew, though, was that he was a broken, hurting man, and she'd heaped on that hurt by treating him as second class, the exact same way people had treated her for years. You'd think she'd know better.

"Back to my question. How long have you been working on vehicles?"

He shrugged. "Just since I've been at Our Home." A smile slowly edged up his lips. "They call me an engine whisperer. I like that."

"Nice. And you can diagnose what's wrong with the bus that fast?" She snapped her fingers.

"Well, I haven't exactly diagnosed anything yet. Not until it cools down." He pulled out his phone—the latest iPhone model—and checked the time. "Let's give it another ten minutes, then we'll see."

She couldn't afford a new iPhone. How could he?

Again, she wanted to know much more than she deserved to know. Yet, here she was stuck with him by the roadside. She could be snobby and ignore him or be friendly and try to get to know him better.

Her stomach let out a low rumble.

Or she could get snacks for the guys and avoid conversation altogether. She got up and wiped grass and dirt off her jeans. "I'm getting a water. You need something to drink? Eat?"

"Sure. I'll have a water and a banana."

The guy ate healthy too. Not yet had she seen him with junk food, whereas, that was half of what Nate ate. "I'll be right back." She hurried onto the bus and found Nate seated by the table, doing something on his phone while eating, and not looking one bit worried. Huh. What if this breakdown was a several-day, several-hundred-dollar repair? Then what would they do?

"Need something?" He glanced up at her and spoke with his mouth full.

"Just checking to see if you wanted something to eat, but it looks like you're covered." She walked past the dinette and Jet's bed and slipped behind the curtain. She grabbed a cold bottled water from the fridge and restocked the fridge with a couple of warm bottles. Then she broke off a couple of bananas and returned to Jet.

She took a deep breath and sat beside him again. She could do this. She could be civil to him and not be afraid of him or angry with him. After handing Jet his water, she took a long swig of hers.

He nudged her foot with his, and she jumped. "Tell me your story. What's out in New York that we're going to?"

"A job," she said as her heart rate slowed to normal. A job she was terrified of. Who was she to think she could be a mold design engineer at a New York company? She was Little Miss Nobody from Podunk, Minnesota.

"That's all you're going to give me? And I thought women liked to talk."

She laughed. "Not this one. Especially about myself." She ran her hands over her jeans. "I got a job as a mold design engineer for a company that makes molds."

"Huh?"

That was the usual response. "Not mold, like the mold in

your house, but a mold that will shape high-tech products. This company makes molds for medical equipment, automotive parts, aerospace parts, etc. and I'm going to be designing the mold."

"Impressive."

"Thanks." She shrugged but had to admit she was blown away by the opportunity. To think that she was going to have the privilege of designing new creations! If she was this excited about designing automotive parts, just imagine how excited God had to be when He designed Earth and the animals and people populating it.

And He was still molding her broken parts. The proof was sitting right beside her. No doubt, Jet coming along on this trip was not a coincidence.

"And you're staying with Nate's aunt and uncle?"

"Sort of. They had an unfinished area above their garage, so when I graduated—"

"Nate said you graduated top of your class."

"Nate exaggerates." She wasn't the top grad, but she had graduated Summa Cum Laude. She'd worked her tail off for those grades.

"Sorry I interrupted. Mother always said I was rude."

A shimmy zinged up her spine with Jet's emotionless statement. That was more than a mother criticizing her child. Was that why he'd bullied her all those years ago? "Oh my gosh, Jet. I love that you're curious and ask questions. When you ask people about themselves, it's telling them they're important to you, so always feel free to ask, even if I'm not good at answering."

He looked at his phone again, a smile evident on his face. "About that garage . . . "

"Well, it's a huge three-car garage, and there was plenty of space above it for an apartment, so when I graduated, they told me to look for work out by them. Ricky's got connections, and he gave me some tips for interviewing, and I managed to get a job out there. Turns out, they'd spent the winter adding the apartment, assuming I'd be moving, so now it's ready for me. A one-bedroom with a full bath, full kitchen, living room, and even a little office nook."

"But do you have to go through their place to get to your apartment? That could get awkward, especially if you bring a boyfriend home."

Her cheeks must have turned an apple red, they got so hot. "Um, well, I do have my own entrance, but I won't be bringing any guys home."

"Oh, I get it. You're like Nate. Waiting for marriage."

"That's the plan. It's the way God wants it."

He snorted. "So those of us who haven't followed *His plan* are out of luck."

"Oh no. That's not what I meant at all. As much as I try to do things right all the time, let's face it, I fail on so many levels every day. Like how I've been rude to you. That's not showing Jesus to you at all. The thing is, Jesus died for us, so even though I mess up all the time—everyone does—we're forgiven. It's the most amazing love ever."

"You're saying He died for me too."

"Absolutely."

He laughed. "Sounds like a fairy tale to me."

"I agree. It's too fantastic to be believable, but yet I believe it with all my heart."

"If that's what makes you happy." He checked his phone again then nodded toward the bus. "Should be cool enough now."

He got up and sauntered toward the bus. At least he'd listened to her. Yes, Jesus' story could sound like a fairy tale, but it was true.

She wouldn't be any help with the bus, so she remained seated in the grass and lifted a prayer for Jet that he would open his heart to God. She prayed that she would continue to offer him grace, when all she wanted to do was scream at him for making that middle school year a living nightmare that impacted her to this day. Insecurity and fear always seemed to be hovering around the corner, waiting for a sliver of an opening, and they'd worm their way into her psyche if she let them.

"I think I found it!" Jet yelled from beneath the hood.

Nate leaped out of the bus and joined Jet by the engine.

"Look at this." Jet held up a rusty screw-in cap of some sort. "No way could this puppy hold pressure in." He looked down the road then at Nate. "See if you can find an auto parts store close."

Nate pulled his phone from his back pocket and scrolled through it. "Here." He pointed to the screen. "If we continue up this exit and take a right, there's a place a few miles down the road."

"Sounds good." Jet screwed on the poorly-functioning cap. "We should be able to drive that far without a problem. An auto parts store, or even a mechanic, should have a cap."

"I actually might have one." Nate gestured to the back of the bus.

"Seriously?" Jet followed behind.

Okay, something was fishy here. If Nate had a new radiator cap, why wouldn't it be on the bus already? She followed the guys to see what they'd find. Nate pulled out a cardboard box filled with what looked like random small auto parts.

"These are parts Gregg had lying around his garage. I think he salvaged them from beaters. He said you never knew when one of these would come in handy."

The guys dug through the box, laying the various parts out on the floor of the bus.

"This might work." Jet grabbed a twist-on cap, then he picked up another part that looked like it had a spring wrapped around it. "And while we're in there, let's check out the thermostat too."

"Lead the way." Nate followed Jet to the front of the bus, but she swore she saw a satisfied grin on his face, rather than a hopeful or relieved grin. Yep, something smelled fishy indeed. If Nate had planned this breakdown to help build up Jet's self-esteem, it was working.

Jet tinkered on the engine for a few minutes, then asked Nate to start it up while Jet stood watching. She stared at it too, but she understood Greek better than an engine. If she was going to be designing parts for vehicles, that had better change. Jet mumbled something about the fans working, then he slammed the hood shut and gave Nate a thumbs-up.

"It's fixed, just like that?" She followed Jet into the bus.

He plopped down on a dinette bench, doubt filling his face. "We'll know soon enough."

"Well, you should be proud of yourself for fixing what you did."

"Listen to Lauren," Nate called from the driver's seat while the bus idled on the side of the road. "I wouldn't have had a clue what to look for. You feel up to driving yet?" Nate gestured to the wheel.

"Be glad to." Jet hurried to the front and claimed the driver's seat. Nate gave some general directions, then joined Lauren at the dinette, humming in that horrible off-key way his family was cursed with.

"You're looking mighty satisfied." She swayed as the bus pulled out onto the road.

"We passed our first hurdle." He raised his Pepsi can in the air.

"Hmmm." She wasn't going to mention her suspicions.

"What does that mean?"

She shrugged. "Just that it's awfully convenient for you to have the exact parts needed for the repair."

"Why would I sabotage The Draken? This is my baby."

"My question exactly."

"Whatever." He left her sitting at the dinette and took the captain's chair where he started a conversation with Jet, effectively ending her inquisition.

Had Nate orchestrated the need for repair to boost Jet's self-esteem? If so, that was a pretty selfless thing to do, and she was mighty proud to call him brother.

Chapter Six

*L*auren would not be a wimp today. She awoke to the sun streaming in through her window, but she didn't feel very rested. After arriving in Sandusky late last night, sleep hadn't come easily for her. On top of sleeping in an unfamiliar bed and her concern for Jet's mental health, her mind was abuzz, keeping sleep at bay.

Did someone need to be well-rested to go on amusement park rides? No doubt, Nate wouldn't take "being tired" as an excuse for chickening out of going to the park today. If she did tire of hanging around with the guys, she could walk from the park to the bus.

While Nate and Jet slept—their snores gave that away—she got up and retrieved her suitcase from the back. Maybe if she got to the showers early, there wouldn't be a line.

Ha! No such luck. The showers were full, and a line of women, teens, and children were already waiting. It seemed everyone but Nate and Jet awoke early.

She got in line, and her mind returned to the ruminating that had kept her awake the night before.

She couldn't figure out Jet. Yesterday, he'd been great. When the bus overheated, he'd coolly pulled off the road, assessed the situation, and taken care of it. But his outburst at the campground the night before was worse than his behavior had been back in middle school. Did little bullies always grow up to be bigger bullies?

Then last night, she'd even eavesdropped on a conversation between Nate and Jet about tools in their mental health toolkit.

If someone asked her what her most important tool was, she'd have to say the Bible. That was a given. But if she went deeper than that, pulled tools for her personal toolkit from the Bible, the words "Fear not" came to mind. Someone had once told her that the Bible had 365 mentions and variations of "fear not," one for every day of the year. Another acquaintance disagreed and said in their research they only came up with just over a hundred. Still, if God exhorted his people to "fear not" over a hundred times, that meant something.

Maybe she needed to begin each day with a "Fear not" verse. Assuming there were just over a hundred mentions, that meant that in a year's time, she'd read each verse at least three times.

While waiting in line, she did a search on her phone for "fear not" and came up with several helpful sites, many of which listed the first verse in Genesis 15:1: "Do not be afraid, Abram. I am your shield, your very great reward."

And Abram had something to be afraid of. God had come to him in a vision and spoken to him. That would freak her out. And then, God told this elderly man that he'd be the father of nations. Yeah, that would be worth fearing. But God . . .

God is the reward and shield.

Knowing that should buoy her through the day. Maybe, just maybe, she'd gather the courage to ride one of those monster coasters. Nate would be mighty proud of her.

She could do it. She could do it.

But what about spending the day with Jet? A man who still stirred anger in her. Last night she'd read in Ephesians, ""In your anger, do not sin": Do not let the sun go down while you are still angry, and do not give the devil a foothold."

Oh boy, she had given the devil a foothold, hadn't she?

Jet had claimed he was a work in progress.

Obviously, he wasn't the only one.

Through her entire shower, she continued psyching herself up. She was not going to be a fraidy-cat today. She wasn't going to let her past with Jet ruin the day.

And then she strode back to The Draken, climbed the stairs and stood at the front of the bus, hands on hips, and connected gazes with both Nate and Jet.

"I'm going to ride today."

Nate stared at her as if she had been dunked in blue paint, then he pretended to clean out his ears. "I'm sorry, I don't think I heard you right. You, Miss I-Hate-Roller-Coasters, want to go on rides today?"

She lifted her chin. "Bring 'em on."

Nate returned a toothy grin and he laughed, rubbing his hands together. "What are we waiting for?"

She strode alongside the guys as they joined throngs of others on the path to the park, but her heart was beating faster than the high-as-a-skyscraper, more-tangled-than-a-pretzel coasters zooming in front of her. Was she crazy? This wasn't about conquering fear. This was insanity.

Her breaths came out in quick stabs. She forced her feet to move forward and lagged behind the guys. Maybe what she needed was a paper bag.

Nate turned and started walking backward. "You coming?"

"I, uh . . . " She gulped.

Those coasters back home in Minnesota had nothing on these. Hoo boy. What had she gotten herself into?

He flapped his arms like a chicken. "We won't force you."

"Jerk!" She wrinkled her nose.

He just grinned. "There's no reason to be scared."

Grrr. He might as well be quoting the Bible. Chances were, if Jesus was standing in front of her right now, He'd mimic Nate and tell her, "There's nothing to be afraid of. I've got this."

But, really, Jesus was not talking about roller coasters.

Or was He?

Nate nodded to Jet. "Let's give her a hand."

They came back and looped their arms with hers. One strong guy on each side of her. What was there to be afraid of? Maybe today was a day of stepping out in faith, even in a small way.

Riding roller coasters with the man who'd help instill that fear in her? Whom she felt a visceral anger toward?

It was a feeling, and feelings weren't wrong. Actions were. And she was tired of behaving like a grump around Jet. Her dad . . . actually, all her dads, including Nate's father and Sheila's husband, would be mighty disappointed in her behavior on this trip. Today, that was coming to an end.

With God holding her hand, she could do it.

She raised her chin and strode forward with the guys. "Let's do it."

With her heart pounding, she led them to the front gate where they purchased their tickets. She then followed her nose into the park, the scent of cotton candy and hot dogs and fudge made her already-upset stomach churn even more.

She came to a stop at a crossroads and looked back at the guys. "Which way?"

"You ever been on a coaster?" Jet asked while studying a park map.

"It's been years." Back in high school, she'd gone to a Minnesota amusement park with her dad. He'd been the one person who could get her to step out of her safety box.

"Then we'll start with something small." He folded the map and pointed.

But she ignored him. "No, I vote we start with something big, that way, even if it scares the pants off me, I can say I did it."

"You sure?" Nate grinned. He was enjoying this far too much.

"No, so we better hurry before I change my mind."

"This way." Jet took off, and her reluctant feet followed behind.

"I can do this. I can do this. I can do this." She repeated

over and over again as the coaster entrance loomed nearer. This one not only went a zillion miles into the air and had more curves than the infinity symbol, but you rode on your stomach.

Her bravado fled as the coaster made its climb up that first hill, the riders on their stomachs, faces toward the ground. "I think I changed my mind." She turned to head out of the ride queue.

But Nate grabbed her arm. "If you don't do this now, you'll regret it."

"No I won't. I'll never regret staying alive."

"C'mon, Lauren." Jet leaned close and whispered in her ear. "I'm scared too."

She looked at him, her eyes wide, and he nodded.

"Fine. But if I die, I'm coming back to haunt both of you."

"Worth it!" Nate high-fived with Jet.

A couple of teens squeezed past them.

And Jet grabbed the arm of one of the teens. "No butting in line."

Oh no, here we go again. Lauren laid a hand on Jet's back, hoping to diffuse the situation before it got out of control. "Just let it go, Jet."

He turned to her, his jaw clenched. "But they—"

"Isn't there a tool Casey'd have you pull out?" Nate stepped between Jet and the kid. "Didn't you say something about a rake?"

Jet released the teen's arm. Blowing out a breath, he nodded. "Recognize the warning sign. My whole body's tense."

"Mine is too, buddy. What's next?"

Jet took a step forward. "Assess the situation. I'm blaming the kids for butting in line. Which they did."

"Yep, you're right." Lauren moved forward in line so more rude guests wouldn't take advantage of them. The guys followed. "And that made you angry, right? Just so you know, it made me angry too."

"Really? You don't show it."

"Well, I ask myself if it's worth it to make a big stink out of it, and honestly, they're not worth ruining my day over." She needed to personally take those words to heart. Yeah, Jet had bullied her in the past, but it was in the past. Today, he was working on becoming a better person.

Screams overhead interrupted their talk. If Jet could be talked down from reacting to these smart-aleck kids, she could ride this coaster.

"How are you supposed to deal with the anger?" Nate took a step forward until he was directly beneath the track. No way was she standing there with him.

"Um, well first, I identify my trigger." Jet held his hand like pointing a gun. "I want to control their actions, but I can't by bullying them. Or if I try to bully them, nothing good comes of it."

His recognition of that fact almost made her tear up. Yeah, Jet had issues, but he was fighting through them, and that took tremendous courage. Rather than fearing him or being angry with him, maybe it was time she started learning from him. She asked the next question, wanting the answer as much for herself.

"Since bullying isn't the answer to dealing with your anger, what is?" She spread her arms across the queue, preventing more kids from sneaking through.

He peered upward, and his eyes worked back and forth. "RAIC," he said mostly to himself, then smiled. "I got it. C. That's the *Cool Down* tool. Take deep breaths. Count to ten. Picture myself in my favorite place. Stuff like that."

"Is it working?" Nate stepped out from beneath the track.

Lauren hustled through and joined him.

"Yeah, it is." A smile blossomed on Jet's face as if he realized that he was conquering his demon. "It's working."

Thank you, Jesus! Situation number one was diffused. How many more would they face today? She shook off the idea. Thinking about that was inviting trouble, and riding this whacked-out coaster was trouble enough.

She ducked as the coaster roared over the pretzel-like track above them. Even though the temps were in the low sixties, she was perspiring. But she wasn't going to back out. If Jet could deal with his anger, she could face down her fears.

Besides, if she wanted a peaceful road trip, she couldn't chicken out now. Nate would never let her live it down.

All too soon they were at the front of the line, and then she was ushered into a seat where she was strapped in so tightly, from foot to head, she couldn't breathe.

Or maybe she forgot how to breathe.

A crackly voice came over the loudspeakers and suddenly the seats raised up then tipped, and she was facing the ground. She clutched the restraints so tightly her knuckles turned white, as if holding on would keep her from flying off into oblivion. Why was she doing this? Just to prove she wasn't a wimp? Not worth it. Not worth it, at all. She was going to pee her pants, and then she'd be a laughing stock, and she'd be bullied all over again. *Please, God, help me survive.*

Then the cars began to move, and the coaster clanked forward and then up a hill. All she could see was the ground slowly pulling away from her and massive, spider-like legs supporting the ride. If she threw up right now, at least she wouldn't hit anyone.

Maybe the tools Jet used to still his anger would work for her.

Close her eyes. Take deep breaths. Count to ten. No, make that a hundred.

Still, she felt the slow ascent as the chain clanked above them. Would they never reach the top?

And then the ride jerked to a stop, leaving them suspended too-many hundred feet above the ground. Voices around her grew shrill, and she dared to open an eye.

Then wished she hadn't.

The ride had stopped, and they were stuck in the middle of the air with her body parallel to the ground!

Chapter Seven

*L*auren clamped her eyes shut. Her heart rate quickened, and her breaths started coming in frantic waves.

"What?" Jet squeaked beside her, evidencing more than a tinge of fear in his voice. Other voices in front of and in back of them joined in, sharing the fear, while others were joking and making light of the situation.

Nothing about this was worth joking over.

"You doing okay, Lauren?" Nate's voice was a sea of calm. How could he do that when they were trapped a hundred-some feet in the air?

"No." A tremble filled her whisper.

"Remember what we were just talking about with Jet? How he could deal with his anger?"

She nodded as much as the restraints allowed her. But a lot of good that would do. Nate probably couldn't see her. So she focused on the conversation they'd had down below. She repeated to herself the tools Jet used.

Take deep breaths. Count to ten. Picture yourself in your favorite place.

Sure, she could do all that. If her feet were on the ground.

Her eyes still closed, she concentrated on her breathing, taking intentionally deep breaths and letting it out slowly.

That didn't help at all.

Then what?

Counting.

No, she had a better idea.

She began singing the ABCs out loud, so she wouldn't hear the anxiety from the other passengers. Jet joined in, followed by Nate. His voice was so awful, it made her laugh. Others joined in, making an odd but beautiful choir, and she dared to open her eyes.

Yes, she was suspended in the air.

But she was safe.

The bars and straps restraining her barely let her bat an eyelid, much less fall. She was going to be okay. And frankly, if something went horribly wrong on the ride—which it wouldn't—she'd be with Jesus.

I can do this. I can do this. I can do this.

The ride jerked, and just like that, they were moving again. She kept her eyes open and like Nate, she even released her death grip on the restraints, allowing herself to feel the freedom of flying through corkscrews, over and beneath the track. This was freedom: facing her fears—with her eyes wide open—and conquering them.

All too soon, the ride returned to its home and came to a stop. Their seats flipped upright. Her heart was still beating furiously, but more from fun than fear.

She'd conquered that ride! And she'd even go again. Finally, she understood the adrenaline rush people got from moving out of their safe zone.

She stepped onto the platform and did a little jig.

"Someone's happy to be on the ground again." Jet put an arm around her shoulders and nudged her toward the exit. "Me too. I practically peed my pants when the ride stopped. If you hadn't started singing . . . "

Nate came around her other side. "Don't worry. We won't push you on any more rides. You slayed this beast, and that's good enough."

She shrugged out of Jet's arm. "Oh, I don't know." She jogged forward and turned around, walking backward. "I think we should give that one a try." She stopped and pointed to the ride that shot its riders straight into the air, then dropped them toward the ground. Just thinking about going on that ride scared her silly, but she was ready to claim victory over that fear.

Jet came to a halt. "You're joking, right?"

"Not at all." She coiled a strand of hair around her finger. Who knew how freeing it was to face down their fears?

"Dang." Jet's eyes grew wide as he watched the rocket ride. "I don't know if I want to go on that."

"Afraid of heights?" Nate socked Jet on the shoulder.

"Terrified, actually."

"Ha, me too." Nate continued toward the ride.

"Me three." Lauren followed Nate.

"Guess I'm going." Jet hurried to walk beside Nate.

Again, her heart was pumping, and it was telling her, *Don't be an idiot.*

"Hey guys, I'm not feeling so hot." Jet slowed, and she

nearly bumped into him. "My heart's pounding."

She would have laughed, but something told her this was serious. She spun around just as he lowered himself to the ground. His skin was way too pale.

"Jet? What's going on?" Nate knelt beside him, took his pulse, then looked back at Lauren with fear widening his eyes. "Get some help."

Before he finished talking, she was off running to a nearby concession stand, her heart pumping faster than it had on the flying ride. She told them to call for medical assistance, and then she hurried back to Jet.

His breaths seemed labored, and perspiration dotted his forehead.

Tears welled in her eyes.

Conquering her fear of roller coasters was one thing—that almost seemed fake right now. This fear for Jet?

That was real, so she did the only thing she could think of.

Pray.

Jet shook his head, trying to get rid of the dizziness. Everything spun around him as Nate lowered him to the ground. He wrapped his arms around his upper body to stop the shivering. Yet he was sweating. Nate was talking to him—what was he saying? His brain was completely foggy. This had happened before, though. What was it the doctor had told him to do?

He slapped the side of his head. *Think, man, think!*

Eat! That was right. Eat. He patted his cargo shorts pockets, searching. Where were they? His hand patted something hard. There?

He tried pulling apart the pocket Velcro, but his fingers wouldn't cooperate.

Nate said something about helping. Fingers that weren't his own opened the pocket and pulled out a tube of . . . What were they?

"How many?" Nate's voice again.

Uh, how many was it? Why was his brain so blurry? Focus, man. Three? Yes, that was it. "Three." He tried to hold up three fingers.

"Here." Nate's fingers were at Jet's mouth, shoving something past his lips. Oh, yes, the glucose tablets. He forced himself to chew and swallow. And waited for the world to come to a halt.

What seemed an eternity later, the spinning slowed, and Nate's and Lauren's concerned faces became clear.

"You okay, man?" Nate studied his eyes.

Jet nodded. "Better. Yeah."

And then medical personnel parted the crowd and rushed toward him. He waved them off. "I'm better. Just a diabetic episode."

The female medic knelt in front of him. "Type 1?"

"Type 2."

"Gotcha. Let's check those blood sugar levels."

Jet frowned, but still held out his hand.

She did a finger prick and seconds later the results showed on the glucometer. "It's seventy-five. Not great."

"But not bad." Jet sucked on his finger. He still wasn't used to this part of diabetes.

"Let's check your other vitals."

"Seriously. I'm okay." Jet drew in a deep breath, wishing the gawking onlookers would mind their own business. "I just forgot to eat this morning, and then the excitement on that last ride . . . "

"Humor me." She took out a thermometer.

"Fine." He allowed the medic to take his temperature, pulse, respiration, blood pressure, and oxygen. All because he'd forgotten to eat this morning. And just like he'd told them, he was okay. Then they advised him to go eat a light snack of a simple and complex carbohydrate with a protein. Maybe a peanut butter sandwich on whole wheat and a glass of milk. Blah, blah, blah. He knew the routine.

Finally, the medics left, as did the crowd. Man, he was an idiot. He knew not to skip meals, and to listen to what his body was saying. But that last ride had given him mixed signals.

"Dude, you scared us crazy." Nate sat beside him on the curb. "Why didn't you tell us you have diabetes?"

Jet looked off at the ride they had been running toward. His blood sugars had fallen like those riders. "I don't know. Guess I don't want to make a big deal out of it." Not like his mother had. One more flaw in her defective son. *Shut up!* He mentally yelled at those finger-pointing voices in his head. Yes, he made mistakes, but so did everyone. He was not defective. He was not worthless. He was not an idiot.

He pushed off the ground. "I should get something to eat."

"I'm assuming that wouldn't be a hot dog, right?" Nate elbowed him.

Jet managed a smile. "Probably not the best idea right now."

"What can you have?" Lauren walked alongside him.

"Lots of stuff. I'm actually hungry for a walnut salad and yogurt right now."

"Salad? Dude! At a fair?"

"Right? It's all a change in mindset." He tapped his temple. The change in mindset about what he ate wasn't that different from the change in how he thought of himself or how he reacted to stressful situations. If he could alter his eating habits, it shouldn't be that difficult to change his emotional habits. But not all *shouldn'ts* faced reality.

"So where do we get healthy food at an amusement park?" Nate pulled his map of the park from his back pocket. "Is that even a thing?" He jerked to a stop and looked at Jet with a horrified expression. "Does that mean you can't have cotton candy?"

"I shouldn't." Although he was feeling much better right now. Treating himself once in a while was okay, but after an episode, he'd better not.

"Dude! That's the worst thing ever."

Jet laughed. "Tell me about it. I love cotton candy and pronto pups and greasy burgers."

Lauren held her map out front and pointed. "There are

actually a number of places with salads and veggie burgers."

Nate slapped a hand to his heart. "Just kill me now. Veggie and burger should not be used together. It's wrong on so many levels."

"You are such a child, Nathan Brooks." Lauren laughed and pointed to a place on the map that was just ahead of them. "This place has junk food for Nate, and healthy options for me and Jet."

"Fine. Go ahead and show me up." Nate pointed to himself. "I can eat healthy too, you know. Just watch." He lowered his voice to a whisper. "Don't tell Mom, though. She'll expect it from me every time."

Lauren zipped her fingers across her mouth. "Not a word to her, but I might have to tell your Aunt Sheila. She'd love to serve you tofu and kale and seaweed."

"Right. And then Uncle Ricky and I would be making a trip to the local pizza joint, so we don't starve."

"Guys. That's enough." Jet held out his hands. Although he did enjoy listening to their banter. What would it have been like to have a sibling to fight with? Maybe take some of the heat off of him? Maybe he'd find out soon. "Actually, a meat-covered pizza wouldn't be a bad idea either."

"You sure?" Nate studied the map. "We don't want another episode."

"Positive."

"That's the place." Lauren pointed ahead.

Nate slapped Jet's back. "No more secrets, okay? Lauren and I are here for you."

"I'll be an open book." Except for that one detail he'd confirmed last night, that wouldn't just affect their road trip. It could affect Jet's entire life. In a few more days he'd know for sure.

Chapter Eight

*J*et waited while Nate unlocked The Draken. Night had fallen an hour or so ago, and Lauren had returned from the park a few hours earlier. Still, Jet was impressed that she'd stayed with them that long.

He dropped off his bag of souvenirs, and nature called him to the men's room. That was what he got for drinking so much water all the time. Giving up pop hadn't been easy, but his health was more important. Today's episode had been a blip, so tomorrow he would do better. The body was amazing, really. Today it had reminded him not only to eat, but to eat the right things. Just like his body warned him of potential angry outbursts.

From now on, he'd pay closer attention to what his body was telling him.

Like right now, it was yelling at him to find a restroom.

He slipped quietly past Lauren who was curled up asleep on the dinette bed. She'd been a trooper today, going on everything he and Nate wanted to ride. From what he could tell, she'd enjoyed it.

Somehow, she'd seemed different today. More open.

Less . . . afraid maybe? Especially after that crazy first ride. She'd freaked out less than he had. Even with his hypoglycemic episode, today had been fun.

Nate followed him out of the bus to the restroom. Then it was time to stretch out the legs. He walked from the men's room with Nate and pointed toward Lake Erie which surrounded the campground. "I need a bit of alone time, if that's okay."

"No problem. I'm gonna get a fire going in the pit, make some supper."

"Good idea. I'll be back soon."

Jet walked past several little cabins, stretching out his muscles along the way, to the shores of the great lake. Trees were scarce in the area, and lights were lit in most of the RVs and cabins, so he had a lack of privacy, but the lapping water usually helped him block out the sounds of people around him.

Once he felt he was secluded enough, he pulled out his phone and started dialing.

Then stopped.

What if his father didn't want to hear from him? What if the man's wife or other kids answered? What if Jet had the wrong information, and this wasn't his father's number?

Could he deal with his father's rejection?

He sat down on the sandy beach and stared up at the cloud-covered sky that looked as if it was ready to pour rain any second. The wind had picked up as well, bringing that rain-is-coming scent with it.

Jet had had too much rain in his life lately, and wasn't

certain he could handle any more, so he tucked the phone into his back pocket. Lightning flashed in the distance. Thunder followed many seconds later. So, the storm was some ways off yet.

This God that Nate and Lauren worshiped, did He create storms? Or did He just allow them in peoples' lives?

"Are You up there?" He gazed upward and followed the rapid movement of clouds. "Do You really care about us?" Nate and Lauren thought so. Another flash of lightning. Thunder answered closer this time. Must be a rapidly moving storm, so he hurried back down the path to the bus.

He jogged past rows of RVs, and heard Lauren say his name. He slipped behind the neighboring camper and peeked around the edge to spy on his friends. Nate had a fire going, and he and Lauren were roasting hot dogs.

"What's up with you and Jet?" Nate rotated the wiener over the fire. "You never did tell me what that freak-out was about back at Our Home. And don't tell me it was nerves. I know you better than that. Today was the first time you seemed comfortable around him."

So, Jet hadn't been imagining things. Nate had noticed her weird vibe around him too.

Lauren tucked her knees close to her body. "I know you hated how insecure I was when I moved in with your family."

"Hate's a pretty strong word."

"Well, that's the way it felt. You were this super-popular guy in a loud, outgoing family, and I was a nobody. At school. At church. Not only did I not know how to be seen, but I was afraid of it too."

"Afraid to be seen? I don't get it." Nate pulled his roasting stick from the fire and rested it on rocks.

A raindrop splattered on Jet's cheek, and he wiped it away, but he didn't move from his hiding place.

"Back when I was in middle school, a few years after my mom died . . ." Lauren wiped below her nose with a napkin. Was she crying? " . . . I was bullied to the point of my dad pulling me out of school."

"Seriously?"

Dread curdled in Jet's stomach and inched up his throat. He wanted to break from the shadows and not hear what Lauren had to say, but his feet were nailed to the ground.

"It was always real covert. Accidentally elbowing my locker door into my face. Sitting behind me in class and cutting my hair, then whispering how ugly I was. Accidentally spilling juice on assignments."

Nate heaved out a breath. "Jet."

She didn't need to answer for Jet to know the truth. He dropped to his knees as memories assailed him. That was the year his dad had abandoned the family, after spending too many years as his mom's verbal and physical punching bag.

But then Jet had taken his dad's place.

He remembered that young girl back in middle school. Super shy. Awkward. Never fought back. Didn't even give him the satisfaction of crying. She'd become his punching bag.

And then she was gone, and some other unassuming girl

had taken her place. And another. His mother was wrong. He wasn't an idiot. No, he was worse. He was a bully who'd made others' lives miserable, so he could feel that he had some control over his life.

Still, that was no justification for his horrid behavior.

More raindrops fell as Jet knelt there. He was a sorry excuse for a human being, and Nate said God loved him? How? When his own mother despised him? When his father had abandoned him, leaving a helpless child alone with his abuser? Where was love in that?

"I wonder where Jet is." Lauren's voice drifted toward him. She sounded concerned. Even with all he'd done to her, she returned kindness. Earlier today they'd laughed together. Faced that crazy ride together. She'd immediately run for help when he collapsed at the park.

"No clue, but he's a big boy." Nate and Lauren gathered their food and cooking supplies. "I think he knows when to come in out of the rain, and if he doesn't, well that's his problem." The siblings disappeared into the bus.

Speaking of returning kindness when Jet had been nothing but wretched, there was Nate who literally ran into a skunk-drunk Jet in a city parking lot. And what did he do? Took him to a place where he shouldn't belong. A place that was for homeless young adults, people who couldn't afford a roof over their heads. That wasn't him. But they took him in anyway.

Was that what love was about?

Thunder responded to lightning, and the clouds wrung themselves out into the air. He drew his drenched hair behind his head and looked up, letting rain wash his face. Was that what God was about?

He had to find out.

He sloshed through the puddles to the bus and opened the door.

Nate laughed from his seat at the dinette, a half-eaten hot dog in a bun on his plate. "Dude, you look like you went swimming, clothes and all."

But Jet remained on the bus steps, dripping. "Why'd you do it, man?"

"Say what?" The teasing smile disappeared from Nate's face.

Jet climbed to the top step. "Why'd you take me in? Why'd Our Home take me in? I have more money in my bank account than you'll ever make. I don't deserve a bed at Our Home."

Nate just sat there, his mouth opening and shutting as if he wanted to speak but didn't know what to say.

"And you, Lauren." He strode the couple feet down the aisle to the dinette, hovered over the table, and growled. "Why are you nice to me?"

Her hands flew to her mouth.

He shoved in beside Nate and slammed clenched fists on the table. "This is important, guys." He leaned toward Lauren. "I heard what you said out there." He stabbed his heart with his finger. "I made your life a nightmare, and yet you call me friend. People don't do that to me. They abandon me. They call me stupid. Worthless. They find out I have diabetes and call me defective. That's what people do to me. That's what my own mother did to me. What's wrong with you guys?"

Lauren blinked, and he saw tears.

"And now I've made you cry." He slammed a fist again. "Once a bully, always a bully."

"Oh, no, no, no." She reached across the table and took one of his damp, balled-up fists. "These tears are for you, Jet. I hate that you've spent your life alone. I hate what others have done to you, and it breaks my heart that you've had to go through that."

"Man, I didn't know." Nate's hand was on his shoulder, pressing his wet T-shirt to his skin. "That's messed up. I'm with Lauren. That stuff should never happen to anyone. To think a mom would treat her kid that way, it burns."

"God's crying for you, too, Jet." Her fingers worked at his, forcing his fist open. "If we've shown love to you, it's only because God loved you and us first."

"Then answer me this: why would He give a kid to parents like that? If He really loved me, why didn't I get folks like yours?"

Lauren shook her head.

Nate said, "That's way above our pay grade."

"We can't answer that." Lauren wrapped her fingers around his. "Like I can't tell you why God took my mom home so young, and then my dad. But the fact that you're on this bus with me and Nate, that's no coincidence."

Jet leaned back and drew a hand through his sopping wet hair.

"And look how you're striving to change." Lauren clung

tighter to him. "Yes, you messed up the other night at the campground, but you want to be better, and you're doing what needs to be done to get better. Not everyone does that."

"Like Mother."

"She's never seen a counselor? Never apologized for anything?" This from Nate.

"Ha! Sure, she's seen a counselor. He's her latest boyfriend. The dude thinks we have the idyllic relationship. Mother's great at wearing masks."

"So, she's hurting as well."

He glared at Lauren. "That doesn't excuse her."

"No, it doesn't."

He tugged away his hand and got up. "If you don't mind, I'm gonna make my bed in the back tonight. I need some time to think."

"Need some help moving boxes?" Nate stood too.

"Nah, I got it."

"One second," Lauren said from behind him. She reached for something and handed him her flower-covered Bible. "If you have questions, this is the best place to go."

He held it loosely, not wanting to show his excitement, and not wanting to get her priceless possession wet. "We'll see." He'd watched her pore through it, write in it, color the pages. This was a cherished item. Was that love?

Hopefully, he'd find out soon.

After changing into dry clothes, he grabbed his blankets and pillows off his bed, walked behind the curtain, made himself a sleeping nook, and began to read.

Lauren joined Nate outside the bus the next morning and handed him a coffee from the camp store. He had a fire going and seemed to be poking at it mindlessly. She hoped he'd gotten more sleep than she had. So far on this trip their nights hadn't been very restful.

Actually, this entire trip had been stress ridden. And she didn't have to drive. Nate must be exhausted. Thank goodness today was a day of rest.

She took a sip of her orange juice, eyeing her brother. When she'd moved in with his family, he'd been the bully, but he'd changed. She'd changed. Jet could change too. Truthfully, in these few days on the bus, he had already changed.

"Have you seen him yet?"

Nate shook his head. "No clue if he's up already and wandering around, or if he's out. Part of me is worried and wants to check on him. The other part is relishing the peace."

"I know what you mean." She looked to the back of the bus. Windows were open, and wind was flapping the curtains. If he was still in there, it was best to keep their voices low. "Did we do the right thing last night? Say the right things?"

He sighed. "I don't know. This is Mom and Dad's department. Uncle Ricky's. They're good at the evangelizing thing. Me? My ministry is picking up strays and dropping them off at Our Home, and then I let others do the hard work."

"Not all the time." She nodded toward the bus. "This one's different. Why?"

He shrugged. "Maybe because his story was different. Even though he was kicked out of his apartment, he could still easily afford a roof over his head. But what he needed more than a roof was a home. He needed Our Home. He needed someone to love him just because. Where do the wealthy go for that?"

"Didn't other Our Home residents object? Most of them are lucky to have had a meal a day before moving in."

He shook his head. "Nobody else knows about his bank account. They just see him as another broken person in need of love."

"And hope."

"Definitely hope."

"Nancy didn't have a fit when you brought him home?"

He laughed. "She has a fit with everyone I bring home, and then she mothers them. And she did bring up his wealth, but I argued that Uncle Ricky always said, money was never to be a consideration. I know he intended that for the poor, but don't the wealthy need to be loved and accepted too? Nancy couldn't argue with that, nor could Uncle Ricky, so Jet stayed."

"You guys talking about me again?" Jet came from the direction of the showers. His hair was damp and combed back, and he had a towel slung around his shoulders. He actually looked refreshed, as if he'd had a good night's sleep.

"Only the good stuff." Nate gestured to one of the collapsible chairs they'd brought along. "It's still a bit damp. We sort of forgot to put them away last night."

"Good thing they didn't blow away." Jet toweled off the chair then sat down.

"Well, a couple got jammed under Draken, or they'd probably be in the next county by now." Nate added a log to the fire and picked up a frying pan that had been lying near his feet. "Want some eggs? Bought 'em this morning. Or can't you eat that sort of thing?"

"Eggs are on the good list, so yeah, I'll take a couple, however you want to make them."

"Lauren?" Nate swung a grate over the top of the fire pit.

"I'll take a couple too."

"Order coming right up." He added butter to the cast iron skillet then placed that on top of the grate. "This makes unbelievable eggs. I tried it out this morning" He smiled at Jet, but the smile instantly drooped. "Oh man, you can't have butter, can you?"

"Don't worry about it. A tiny bit of butter won't hurt me."

"You sure? 'Cause I can dump it out—"

"Cook the eggs, will ya?"

Lauren giggled. This was a much more fun atmosphere than last night. If only they could keep it going.

"Yes, sir." Nate cracked four eggs into the skillet and they instantly sizzled.

"So about last night." Jet spoke, and the air sizzled just

like the eggs.

Lauren reached over and touched Jet's arm. "We're listening.

"I'm sorry I went crazy on you guys. I'm just." He blew out a breath. "Confused."

"Welcome to the world, buddy."

Nate, the goof. Sometimes he was just too glib about things. "What are you confused about?" Lauren made eye contact, hoping to show Jet that what he said was important.

"I had my headphones in when I went to bed last night. Music tends to soothe me, you know?"

"I understand. I'm the same way."

Nate snorted. "Unless the Brooks family is singing."

She shot him a look that hopefully said, "Shut up."

"Anyway, this popular song came on. Well, it used to be popular. 'All You Need is Love' by the Beatles."

"I'm familiar with it." But she had never really listened to the lyrics.

"My mom's a Beatles fanatic, so I heard it all the time, but last night was the first time I'd listened to it, and I don't get it." Jet now focused solely on Lauren.

"What do you mean?"

"It just repeats the title over and over and the lyrics say nothing. I listened to it, hoping it would tell me what love is. The song says I need it, but it didn't tell me what love looks like. And so many of the songs I listen to are all about sex or making out. Movies and TV shows, the same thing. But if that's all there is to love, and if that's all we ever need . . . I don't know, it just feels real shallow."

Lauren felt like doing a little jig. *He gets it, God.* Who wouldn't be confused looking at the world's definition of love? She pointed to Nate cooking eggs over the fire, eggs that looked almost done. "Love looks like that. Nancy and Gregg and all the volunteers at Our Home? That's what love looks like. You sitting down to talk to me in a roadside ditch. That's what love looks like."

"Mmmm." His mouth twisted as if he were confused.

How could she explain better? Well, maybe she couldn't explain better, but she had a Book that did. "There's even more." She held up a finger and rose to retrieve her Bible from the bus, then remembered she'd loaned it to Jet. "Would you mind getting my Bible?"

"No problem." Jet jogged toward the back of the bus.

And Lauren lifted up a silent prayer for help.

"Now who's being the evangelist?" Nate lowered his voice and glanced toward his bus.

Lauren shrugged. "I'm just answering questions."

"And I'm being a pain in the butt." Nate scooped two eggs each onto two paper plates.

"Uh-uh. Didn't you hear me say it? You look like love."

Nate snorted. "Right. Tell that to all my ex-girlfriends."

"There are a few." Lauren giggled.

He pretended to throw a punch.

"What are you doing?" Jet roared toward them from the bus.

"Whoa, calm down there, Raging Bull. We were just having some sibling fun."

Jet looked to Lauren for confirmation.

She nodded. "We were goofing around. Love looks like that too." She picked up one of the plates and handed it to Jet. "Love also lets you eat your eggs while they're warm, if you don't mind listening."

"Go ahead." He must have been starving because he attacked the eggs.

She said a quick prayer of thanks then opened her Bible. She was far from an expert on love, and she knew she'd miss important things, but God would fill in the cracks. "One of the most popular chapters in the Bible is 1 Corinthians 13. It tells us outright what love is. It's patient, kind. It doesn't envy or boast. It isn't proud. It doesn't dishonor things. It's not self-seeking or easily angered—"

"Ha, guess I failed that one."

"Yes, you did. And I have too. All of these. But listen to what comes next. Love keeps no record of wrongs." Her eyes focused on his. "None."

"Wow."

"I know, right?" Something niggled at her then. If love kept no record of wrongs, then why had she held on to Jet's bullying? She closed her eyes and the Bible fell to the ground. Sure she'd stuffed away memories—even hatred— of Jet, tucking them deep inside her, but she'd never freed them. She'd never forgiven him, and that unforgiveness had festered inside her for years. Tears trickled down her cheeks, and sharp pain twisted her stomach. Releasing Jet, forgiving him would be like saying goodbye to a long-time friend.

"You okay, Lauren?" Jet. She felt a hand on her back, the hand of the enemy.

She nodded but couldn't speak.

Unforgiveness had been the real enemy. It had been a fiend stealing away her confidence, replacing it with a spirit of fear. It had stolen away her freedom to be the glorious person God created her to be.

"Lauren, you're scaring us." Nate pressed a hand to her shoulder, drawing her away from her pondering.

She shook from his grip, then looked at Jet. But that wasn't enough. She got down on her knees beside her fallen Bible and looked up at him, begging God for the right words. "I need to apologize, Jet."

He waved his hand. "No you—"

"Please. It's important." She inhaled to the count of four and let it out just as slowly, all the while keeping her gaze locked on Jet. "When I first saw you back at Our Home, I had a panic attack. All the memories from years ago rushed at me, and . . . and I became afraid and angry."

"I'm sorry, Lauren, I wish I could take everything back. I wish I hadn't hurt you or anyone else, but I can't undo it."

She took his hand. "I forgive you, Jet. And I should have said those words years ago. The thing is, real love keeps no record of wrongs, yet I've stored your wrongs inside for years. Yes, I kept them under lock and key, but they always manage to break out, and never in a good way. I thought that you coming along on this road trip was God's way of reaching you, and that may be true, but He's used it to reach me, to show me that I've been unforgiving, and He's shown me how harmful that is. I forgive you, Jet. Can you forgive me?"

He just stared down at her, then eked out the words, "Forgive you?"

"For holding on to hate. Can you forgive me?"

He looked up at the sky that held no remnants of last night's storm. "This is love?"

"One way to show it, yes."

He smiled down at her. "I think I'm getting it."

Yes, Jet was beginning to understand what love really was, but did that include reconnecting with his father? He threw out his garbage then pulled his phone from his pocket. "I need to make a call."

"Make it fast." Nate discarded his paper plate then rubbed his hands together. "Roller coasters are awaiting."

"No problem." Jet hurried to the lake and dialed his father's number. Voice mail picked up, and a familiar voice spoke, setting off a war in his stomach. He could cop out again, but he'd never forgive himself if he did.

He cleared his throat and forced out the words. "Dad, this is Jet—Jethro. I'm gonna be in town tomorrow, and I'd love to get together."

He left his phone number and hung up, then looked to the sky. "Um, God, if You really are there, if You really listen, if You really answer prayer like Nate and Lauren say You do, could You please have my dad call me back?"

Chapter Nine

Jet rejoined Nate and Lauren, vowing to himself that he wouldn't let waiting for his father's return call ruin his day. He pointed to the park not too far away from their parking spot and grinned at Nate. "Time for some fun!" He glanced at Lauren, who was settled in a chair on The Draken's side yard, a strip of grass the length of the parking space. "Sure you don't want to join us?"

"I had enough excitement yesterday. You two go have fun."

He checked his back pocket for his phone as they jogged through the campground lot. If his father called, he didn't want to miss it.

Maybe Jet would finally be welcomed back into his family, and he'd get to be the wise older brother to his father's other kids.

Stop it, Jet! Worrying about the phone call or getting his hopes up too high would only ruin his day.

He and Nate jogged past families making their way to the park entrance. Happy families who clearly liked to spend time together.

Was it possible to forgive if the person wasn't around to tell them? Could he forgive his father for abandoning him? What if his dad wouldn't accept forgiveness? Nate could probably answer, but he'd rather ask Lauren. Anything to spend some time with her. She was the first girl—woman—ever to make him believe in himself.

And it didn't hurt that she was rather cute, too. No way would he admit that to Nate. Jet would never hear the end of it.

They reached the entrance and the worker scanned their tickets.

Time to have fun!

"Want to start big?" Nate pointed to a coaster that went straight up—seriously!—into the air. The brochure claimed it went up 420 feet. Crazy! Yesterday, he'd been terrified before the ride began, but the adrenaline rush afterwards made it worth it. "Or do you want to build up to it?"

Jet nodded to the crazy-tall coaster. "Why don't we start with a bang, and then go to the mild rides and work back up to the big ones? Sort of like how *Jurassic Park* begins."

"It's a plan." They ran toward the queue.

Not much of a plan since he left his stomach at the peak of that coaster. Maybe they should have waited a little bit longer after breakfast to hit the park.

"Go again?" Nate gestured toward the line that wasn't too long yet.

"Hey, why not? I need to go get my stomach anyway."

Nate laughed. "Me too!"

So they rode that coaster again. By closing, they'd hit

every other ride in the park a second, sometimes a third time. If he didn't go on another ride the rest of the year, he'd be fine.

The sun was just beginning its descent when they exited the park and began their journey back to the campsite alongside hundreds of other campers and hotel patrons. He'd enjoyed spending time with Nate, but a sunset should be shared with someone special. Tomorrow they were heading to the Hershey, Pennsylvania, area. Since the drive would be over seven hours, they didn't have plans for the evening.

Unless his dad called back.

Maybe he and Lauren could . . .

Should he ask Nate about her? Or would that be too weird? Not like Nate was her dad or anything, yet the guy was protective of her. But if Jet didn't ask, he'd regret it, right?

Jet cleared his throat. "Hey, I've a question for you."

"Yeah?"

"Um, Lauren, is she seeing anyone?"

Nate came to a full stop, so Jet had to spin around. His friend's face was screwed up like an old man's. "Seriously? What is it about my friends and Lauren?"

Jet stuck his hands in his pockets. "So she is seeing someone."

"Not right now, but . . . " Nate shook his head. "The guy who helped me with The Draken, he and Lauren dated for a few years. When he got his job in California, and she got hers in New York, they figured it was time to take a break."

"So I can ask her out."

"Really? Lauren?" His nose wrinkled, and he stayed rooted on the sidewalk as people filtered past him, giving the guys strange looks.

"Why not? She's nice, and she's hot, and—"

"You did not just say that, dude. Remember this is my sister you're talking about."

"Sort-of sister."

"Same thing." Nate crossed his arms. "What are you going to do? Take her on one date, then say *adios* when we drop her off in New York?"

"Something wrong with that?"

"Lauren's not that kind of girl."

"Hey, I'm not . . . " He ran a hand through his hair. "That's not my intention. Who knows, maybe that one date would turn into more. I'm looking for work, who says I can't look out east?"

Nate hung his head. "Fine. You're both adults, but dude, if you hurt her . . . "

"She hasn't said *yes*, yet."

"And if she's smart . . . "

Jet pointed toward the campground. "We're blocking the way."

"Because you had to go all weird on me."

They walked side by side toward the bus.

"C'mon, don't tell me if you saw some hot chick—"

"Do I have to remind you, this is my sister?"

"—that you wouldn't be asking her out. You've got a bit of a reputation, not only for bringing home strays."

"I never should have brought you home."

Jet laughed. He was so glad Nate had seen potential in him.

Now he hoped Lauren did too.

She was still seated outside, a book in her hand, but her gaze was on the sunset. That very sun rimmed the edges of her wavy, brownish-red hair with gold. Unlike most women he'd met, she didn't seem overly concerned with being in public without makeup, and he liked the honesty of that. No, not liked, he found it very attractive.

He sauntered toward her and pulled up a chair beside her. "Beautiful, isn't it?"

"Mmmm. I could watch this every night and not get tired of it." She pointed to the horizon. "You want to know what love is? Take a look at that. Every day God paints a different masterpiece for anyone who takes time to notice it. I don't often enough."

"Mind if I watch it with you?"

"I'd love it." She turned her head and looked back at Nate. "You joining us?"

"Naw." So, Nate was being a gentleman. Nice. "I'm gonna review our route for tomorrow. It's going to be a long drive." He rolled his eyes.

"Okay . . . " She turned back to Jet. "What's up with him? Didn't you guys have fun?"

"Oh, man, it was crazy!"

"And no episodes?"

"I'm behaving and paying attention to the warning signs." All of them. No diabetic warnings. No anger warnings. It had been a pretty amazing day.

She patted his arm. "Good for you."

"So, hey, after arriving in Hershey tomorrow, we have no plans for the evening."

"It's going to be our last night, isn't it?" Was that sadness in her voice? He didn't know women enough to read them, but it sure sounded like she was disappointed the road trip was coming to an end. Would she miss him too?

"Well . . . " He rubbed his hands over his khakis. "You don't suppose you'd like to do something with me, would you?"

She shrugged. "I'm sure there's lots to do around there. We'll find something."

"No, I mean, you and me, you know, like a date." Whew, he said it. Why was that so hard? He'd never had difficulty asking girls out before. Did he sound really stupid? He held his breath waiting for an answer.

She dipped her head, then looked up at him, sideways like. "You want to go out with me?"

"Uh, yeah. Since tomorrow is our last night on the road, I thought it would be fun to do something special."

She stared toward the sunset, nibbling on her bottom lip. Then she turned to him, still worrying that lip. "I'd like that, Jet."

Chapter Ten

*M*idafternoon, the bus came to a stop at the campground in Hershey, and Jet flew off before Lauren had a chance to put her book down.

Nate grinned at her from the mirror above the driver's seat. "When ya gotta go . . . "

Well, it had been over three hours since their last stop, just to the east of Pittsburgh. And Jet went through bottles of water like Nate sucked on Altoids. He headed out of the bus too, but Lauren signaled for him to join her at the dinette. "If you're not in a hurry, that is."

"I've got a minute." He slid in across from her. "What's up?"

She looked out the bus window toward the campground's building that housed bathrooms and showers. "I think I made a mistake."

"About Jet?"

She nodded. Her conscience had been talking back to her ever since she'd said 'yes' to him. "I shouldn't have agreed to go out with him tonight. He's got so many issues to work through yet. To be honest, I still have issues with him. And most importantly, he's not a believer."

"You sure you want to talk with me about this? I haven't exactly been a role model for Christian dating."

No, Nate hadn't, which made him the perfect person to talk to. "How do I tell him I've changed my mind without hurting him?"

"Sorry. That's not possible." He looked toward the main building, then back at Lauren. "Why'd you say *yes* in the first place? I admit, that really surprised me."

She shrugged. "I do like him. And even though it's been a short road trip, he seems to have grown so much."

"I agree."

"I've grown too. Truth is, I like him, and in that moment last night, there was a connection I can't explain, so when he asked, it seemed natural to agree to go out with him."

"And you've been regretting it."

"Well, not quite. I admit, I was pretty flattered at first, and excited, and then . . . " Then her conscience kicked in, and she'd been fighting it ever since. Tapping her fingers on the acrylic tabletop, she glanced toward the building again to make certain Jet wouldn't surprise them mid-conversation. "What do I do?"

"How about honesty? When I have issues, my folks tell me to be honest."

But the truth would hurt Jet. Grrr. "How about this? What if I told him I'm flattered he asked me, and I'd be glad to do something with him as a friend tonight since it's our last night on the road, but that's it because he doesn't share my beliefs?"

"Sounds like a plan."

Hopefully, the right plan. "And here he comes. I think I'll shower first, then if you could give us a moment, I'd appreciate it."

He raised his arm, sniffed, and his eyes crossed. "I'm heading to the showers too. We'll get him to watch The Draken, then I'll make myself scarce."

They got up, and Lauren gave him a quick hug. "God knew I always wanted an older brother, and He gave me the best one."

He rubbed his knuckles over his heart. "What can I say?"

They found their shower bags from the storage area and stopped Jet on the way to the building.

"Draken's not locked, so if you could keep an eye on him, I'd appreciate it. Lauren and I are headed to the showers."

"No problem." Jet shot Lauren a flirting glance. "And when you're done, I'll head in. Gotta be my best for tonight."

Oh boy. Telling Jet the truth might be the right option, but it sure wasn't going to be easy. Especially since she was more than flattered that he was interested in her.

Whistling, Jet boarded The Draken. For the first time in his life, things were looking up. He was out from under his mother's thumb. He'd found a career—who knew he'd be good at fixing engines?—that he wanted to pursue, he was learning to deal with his anger and insecurity, and a cute . . . well, more than cute. That an intelligent, caring, humble woman might be interested in a screw-up like him. He'd never been more excited. Or nervous. He had a history of blowing anything that was good for him.

But this was just one date, and then he and Nate would drive home. Maybe, though, if tonight went well, maybe it would become more.

One way to impress her would be to know her Bible better. So far, he'd just skimmed through it, mostly reading her thoughts and notes. She really laid herself bare in the margins. How much of her self-doubt could be traced back to his bullying of her? How many others had he damaged? He was a human wrecking-ball—

No! He squeezed his fingers into his palms. He was not! "Get out of my head, Mother!" he muttered the words but wanted to scream them out. If anyone was a wrecking ball, it had been her.

Now where had he put the book? He checked his bed, where he thought he'd left it, but it wasn't there. He scanned the inside of the bus. There it was on the dinette table.

He picked up the book and his eyes grew wide. Whoa! She'd been busy while he napped the last couple of hours. Sticky flags now stuck out from the pages of the Bible. He scanned through them while returning to his bed. Not only had she marked the pages, she'd written notes on the flags. He sat down and opened the book to a page where #1 was written on the sticky note.

While love can be a feeling or sentiment,
real love is a verb. It's an action.
Read 1 John 3:18.

He searched the page for the verse. It was highlighted, but so were several others on the page. There it was, colored in pink.

Dear children, let us not love with words or speech
but with actions and in truth.

He checked the flags for more numbers. He found #2 in 1 Corinthians, chapter 13. Wasn't that what she read last night?

Real love is selfless. 1 Corinthians 13:4-5.

He read those verses again—the phrase, "it is not self-seeking" was highlighted and underlined.

Love is patient, love is kind. It does not envy,
it does not boast, it is not proud.
It does not dishonor others, it is not self-seeking,
it is not easily angered, it keeps no record of wrongs.

Flag #3 said, "Love is sacrificial" and directed him to 1 John 3:16.

This is how we know what love is:
Jesus Christ laid down his life for us.
And we ought to lay down our lives
for our brothers and sisters.

Seriously? Lay down our lives for others? Was he supposed to take that literally or figuratively? Or both? If that was what love really was, he didn't know if he could do it. He slumped down, his thumb guarding the page. He had so many questions for Lauren and Nate. Hadn't they made sacrifices for him by inviting him on this trip? What about Our Home? He didn't fit in there, yet they'd welcomed him. The least he could do was try to understand what their motivation was.

He searched for #4 among the flags, and his phone rang. He pulled it from his pocket, intending to mute the ringer, but the caller name caught his eye. Wurm Financial Planning. His father's work.

And just like that, tension sizzled in his shoulders. His back. His fingers. He pulled the RAIC tool from his toolkit. As his counselor had taught him—as the diabetic episode showed—his body was telling him something was off-kilter, and he needed to address it, or bad things would happen.

Recognize warning signs. His body was tense, that meant he was building for an explosion.

Assess the situation: His dad's office was on the phone.

The ringer stopped. He knew nothing about the call beyond that, so there was no reason to get worked up.

A ping indicated whoever called had left a message.

Fine. He could deal with that.

Identify the trigger. Fear. Fear that he'd explode around his dad. Fear that his dad wouldn't like him. Fear that he'd hate his dad. Weren't those conflicting emotions? Thoughts? His counselor would remind him that acknowledging his feelings was vital, but feelings do not have to dictate negative actions.

The final step was to *cool down*, but already the tension had vanished. So the RAIC tool was working! Yes! He pumped his fist.

Now to listen to the message with the same measure of calm.

He dialed his voice mail and the message played through the air. "Jethro." The voice cleared. "This is . . . this is your dad. I'm available now if you want to meet. Tonight, I'm busy with family. I'll be at Dino's in Harrisburg for the next hour." He gave the address then hung up.

Jet tried to assess his feelings. No tension knotting his shoulders, so that was good, wasn't it?

His father wanted to meet with him. That was also good. He put the address into his phone GPS, and then the familiar tension awoke. The place was a good forty-five-minute drive from here which meant he had to leave now.

He felt his front pocket for the bus keys. Thankfully, they were there. Going in to the camp building to tell Nate and Lauren would take up precious time he didn't have. A phone call would have to do.

They would understand, wouldn't they?

No time to worry about that.

He started up the bus, headed out of the parking lot, and even lifted a prayer that he'd arrive in time to see . . . confront . . . maybe love his father. Then tonight, he'd treat Lauren to the special kind of night she deserved.

Chapter Eleven

*L*auren dried off then scrunched her wet hair with a dry T-shirt to bring out the curl. For most of the trip, she'd just tied her back in a ponytail, but she wanted to look nice for tonight.

That is, if tonight happened after she gave Jet the "We can only be friends" line, which she needed to do right away. She prayed he'd understand.

She got dressed then applied a bare minimum of makeup for the day, which was more than she'd done for all the previous days on the road trip. Would Jet take that as flirting? She hoped not.

Had he found her Bible while she was in the shower? She'd only just begun marking places for him to read, hoping he'd understand what love really was. She hadn't expected to run across a verse that spoke directly to her. 1 John 4:18 said, "There is no fear in love. But perfect love drives out fear, because fear has to do with punishment. The one who fears is not made perfect in love."

No wonder so many Bible verses commanded followers not to fear. Well, she was working on it. The road trip had helped her out more than she'd imagined.

Finally satisfied with her appearance, she headed back to the bus.

But it wasn't in its parking space.

And Nate stood where The Draken had sat just twenty-five minutes earlier. His hands were clenched into fists, and his face was as red as a ripe tomato.

His gaze connected with hers and he jogged toward her. "You have your phone?"

She felt around her shower bag but knew the answer already. She'd left it on the bus. She always did when she showered. "No. Why?" She looked at the empty space and that familiar fear tumbled in her gut.

"Because . . . " He squeezed the back of his neck with both hands. "Mine's on the bus. The bus Jet just ran off with."

Jet waited about a half an hour before trying to call Nate. He didn't want to leave a message. This conversation needed to happen voice to voice.

He dialed Nate's number and seconds later a familiar ringtone sang from a cubby beside the driver's seat. Seriously? He looked down, beside the seat, and there was Nate's phone.

Don't panic, dude, Lauren has to have her phone. The women he knew never went anywhere without theirs. So, he dialed her number and waited.

Seconds later a song played about being strong in the Lord and not living life in fear. Lauren's tone.

Oh man, oh man, oh man. He pounded the steering wheel as other phone numbers jogged through his thoughts. No way was he calling Our Home. They'd tell him to turn around right now. He couldn't do that. His counselor would say the same, as would anyone else from his new life.

They might be right, but he couldn't miss this opportunity. Once he reached Dino's, he'd look up the campground's number, and talk to Nate.

His GPS warned him of an upcoming turn. One last chance to make a life-altering decision.

Did he take that turn and head toward his father, or did he turn back to the campground before Nate called the cops on him?

Nate wouldn't do that. Would he?

No, he wouldn't. At least not right away. Jet obeyed the GPS and made the turn, aiming toward Harrisburg. That one Bible verse Lauren had pointed out said that love didn't keep a record of wrongs. He'd find out soon enough how much love his friend really had for him.

Lauren had seen Nate angry before, but never like this. He strode into the campground office, the muscles in his face tighter than the hatch on a submarine, and his fists balled even tighter. They'd called Our Home to get Jet's cell number, but no one answered. They were probably having lunch, and phones were all silenced during that hour.

"Any word yet?" Nate said through clenched teeth.

She shook her head.

They'd trusted Jet. Believed in him. Supported him.

How could he do this to them? To himself?

Would she ever see her belongings again? Sure, it was all replaceable, but most of what she'd packed held memories from her parents. That, she couldn't replace.

And Nate certainly couldn't replace the bus he'd spent hundreds of hours on.

She pointed to a table tucked into a corner in the cafeteria and aimed for it, hoping Nate would follow. She sat, and Nate pulled a chair out beside her, its metal feet scraping on the tiled floor echoed throughout the building.

"What do I do, Lauren?" He turned the chair backwards and sat, straddling the back. With a groan, he pounded his fists on the Formica top. "Do we call the police?"

She reached for her phone to check the time, which reminded her again that her phone was on The Draken with Jet. Instead, she squinted at the clock above the check-in desk. He'd been gone almost an hour. Plenty of time for him to be in touch with the campground if he really wanted to. And they'd each called their phones from the campground, letting them ring on. Jet shouldn't be able to ignore them.

"I don't think we have a choice." Although it hurt Lauren to say that. Jet had changed so much. Or rather, they thought he'd changed. Had it all been an act? And for what purpose? It didn't make sense. "The police can track our phones, can't they?"

"I think so." He shrugged. "And it's not like The Draken is easy to hide."

"And it's unforgettable too. People will notice it."

He heaved out a breath then pushed back in his chair. "Let's do this, and hope he has a really good excuse."

Hope and pray.

Where was the GPS taking him? Jet had already bypassed the city and was out in no-man's-land, passing ankle-high crops. Was Dino's a fancy supper club on some river, maybe?

"In five-hundred feet, turn right on Irfan Lane."

Irfan Lane. That was the street Dino's was on. Slowing the bus, he glanced at the dashboard clock. Under ten minutes before his father would leave. Fifty minutes since he'd taken The Draken from the campground. He had to get a call in to Nate before meeting his father, or chances were, he'd be spending the night in the county jail cell.

"Turn right on Irfan Lane."

Jet turned onto a gravel road bordered by trees and slowed even more as stones pelted the bus. Nate wasn't going to be happy about that either.

He drove nearly a mile down the road. Trees on both sides drew closer to the road until it felt like they were squeezing the bus. He couldn't see anything beyond them. Where was this place?

The trees parted, and Jet's chin dropped to his chest as Dino's came into view. This was no supper club, it was a dive. A backwoods bar that only locals would frequent in order to get rip-roaring drunk.

Did that mean his mother had lied all these years? That his father really wasn't wealthy? Was that why she never received child support from him?

He avoided a VW Beetle-swallowing pothole and parked along the back of what Jet assumed was the parking lot, with its mix of gravel and weeds. A half-dozen cars also populated the lot. None a thief would give a second glance to. Jet had always pictured his father driving a Mercedes. What else had his mother lied about?

He made sure he had his phone handy, then got out of the bus and locked it up tight. If Lauren's things were stolen, he'd never forgive himself.

Would she forgive him for standing her up?

Oh, that was the least of his worries.

First, he needed to let Nate and Lauren know what he was up to.

Before going into the bar, he tapped the browser on his phone to look up the campground's number and let loose a curse. No service. Couldn't one thing go right today?

Maybe the bar would have internet service.

Hah! Them serving steak on fine dinnerware would be just as likely.

Was meeting the man who'd walked out on him worth

this?

No. But Jet had come this far already and would regret not taking the next steps, even if the night landed him behind bars. Either for stealing the bus or for planting a fist in his lousy father's face. That would go against everything Lauren had talked about earlier, but it would sure feel good.

He stepped over a trail of cigarette butts and tugged open the heavy door which had a No Smoking sign taped inside the window. The stench of booze nearly knocked him back. Whoa. He'd done his share of drinking and barhopping, but none had smelled this rancid.

Coughing, he entered the dark building and the door slammed shut behind him. He blinked, eyes stinging from smoke. Apparently not all patrons obeyed the No Smoking sign.

Once his eyes focused, he made out the bar straight ahead and trudged over bulging and ripped carpet to get there. The bartender was a young woman, probably around his age, who had more tattoos on her body than she had clothes. With a tatted hand, she shoved a wet rag over the countertop.

"What can I get you?" she asked without looking at him, but as he was the only one near her at the time, he assumed she was talking to him.

"The internet?" It was half joke, half hope.

"Funny guy, huh?"

Right. He looked around the room. Only a few tables were occupied, and in the booth furthest away from the bar, a head rose above the back. Was that him?

"I'm supposed to meet someone here. Name's Reginald Wurm."

She gestured toward the booth with her rag-filled hand. "So you're Reggie's kid. He ordered you a burger."

Reggie's kid. So his father was a regular at this hole-in-the-wall. All this time, Jet had thought he would have been better off living with his father. Hah!

He strode past several mostly-empty tables and rounded the booth. He locked eyes with a man two-fisting what was left of a burger.

An impeccably dressed man who'd barely aged since their last family photo. A man who looked as out of place in this bar as Lauren would.

"You came." He set the burger on the plate. "You going to sit or stare at me?"

Still trying to add up all the incongruities of his executive-looking father in this hole of a diner, he sat down on the vinyl-cracking seat of the booth. He had a million questions for the man. Even more accusations.

But Nate and Lauren took precedence. "Does your phone have service here?"

He stopped midbite. "My phone?"

"I need to contact my friends. I don't have service."

"Well, that's one of the beauties of this place, you see." His father nonchalantly resumed eating. "I get a few minutes peace from the world while enjoying the best burger around."

"Where's the closest place I can get service?"

"Impatient, aren't you? Your mother taught you well."

Familiar tension zinged from his back, down his arms, to his fingers. He could strangle the jerk seated across from him. The letters RAIC floated in front of his brain. *Recognize. Assess. Identify. Cool down.* No doubt, he was stressed, and he wanted to take that out on his father's smug smile.

Which would accomplish nothing good.

"I told my friends I'd be in touch when I arrived." A little lie was okay, wasn't it?

"Then we'll eat quickly." His father stuffed the remainder of the sandwich into his mouth, then wiped a napkin over his lips, all while staring across the table, making Jet want to disappear into the cracked cushion. But Jet returned the stare, refusing to back down. He'd put everything on the line to see his father, he wasn't going to go all wimpy.

And then his dad's eyes softened, and a smile appeared. "You're looking well."

"Thanks. You too." Jet squeezed his fingers on his thighs, trying to ease his tension.

"What brings you out here?" His father dipped a crinkled fry into ketchup.

"A road trip with friends. We just happened to be going through this area."

His father nodded. Was that a tear on his cheek? "I'm glad you did. It's good to see you again."

His tension began to ease away. "You too."

"And your mother? She's well?'

Jet snorted. "Alive and kicking." Almost literally.

And his dad nodded while nibbling on a fry. "I'm sorry, Jethro."

What did he say to that? Thanks? Saying "I forgive you" would be an outright lie. He wasn't anywhere near that yet. Instead he said, "Jet. I go by Jet."

"It fits you." His dad pushed his plate across the table. "Care for a fry?"

"Not really hungry, but thanks."

"You're missing out." He pulled the plate back and slathered a fry in ketchup. "Still work for your mother?"

"Up until a month ago."

"Finally broke loose, huh?"

That was one way of putting it. Jet shrugged. "Guess so."

"And now? What are you doing?"

"Other than driving across the country?" Jet's foot rapped out a beat on the grody carpet, impatient with the small talk. All he wanted to hear was "I love you" or even "I've missed you."

"Hmmm."

Jet swallowed hard. "Um, actually, I was thinking maybe I'd move out here by you. Get to know you, my siblings."

His dad choked, and Jet handed him a glass of water. He drank most of it before setting the glass down. "About that." He stared at the red plastic glass strangled between his hands and cleared his throat. "I've made a good life for myself out here. I'm happy. I've got a wife, one who actually likes me, and a couple of kids who look up to me."

So it was true. Jet had younger siblings. "When can I meet them?"

"Well, here's the thing." His father licked his lips then ran a napkin over his mouth, all while avoiding eye contact. "How much do you need for me to convince you to stay away?"

Jet blinked, trying to make sense of his father's words. "How much?" He shook his head. "What are you talking about?"

"It's like this." His father pulled a wallet from his back pocket and threw a handful of bills on the table. Hundred-dollar bills at that. "I don't need you mucking up my life. You're an adult now, and on your own. Let's just leave things as they are. You go on with your life, and I'll go on with mine, and we'll all be happy."

The slime.

Tension zinged through Jet's body, to his hand. Holding his breath, he balled his hand into a fist.

And Casey's RAIC rushed through his head.

Recognize the warning signs: his blood was pumping hard, every muscle was tense, and relief would only come from connecting his fist to his father's perfect nose. He drew his hand back, even with his shoulder.

Assess the Situation and *Identify the Trigger*. Would he really feel better by punching his dad? Oh yeah, for a whole second. His father was a jerk and deserved to be punched. But after that second, guilt would set in again.

And that action would only compound the trouble he was already in.

Cool down. Taking measured breaths, and picturing in his head a quiet lake, he forced his fist down to the table where he shoved the money back at his father. "I won't be bought."

Wide-eyed, his father stared at Jet, then at the money, then back up at Jet as if in shock, before grinding out through clenched teeth. "I better not catch you anywhere around my family." Jaw set, he greedily snatched up the bills, stood up, and stuffed them into his pocket. "Or else—" His fist went up, mocking the posture Jet had held moments ago.

"Problems, Reggie?" The bartender hollered out, drawing the attention of every other patron in the building.

His father bore his gaze into Jet's, holding his fist even with his chin. "Not if this punk leaves right now and never bothers me again."

"No worries, Pops." Jet got up and glared over at the pathetic excuse for a man. "I don't need filth like you in my life."

Head held high, he strode across the bar, out the door, and to The Draken. So, his mother had been telling the truth all along, that his dad was a worthless excuse for a human being.

He kicked at the gravel and stubbed his toe. Letting out a curse, he limped toward the bus. And to think he'd jeopardized his relationship with Nate and Lauren for this. He'd risked getting kicked out of Our Home for that piece of crud.

He risked going to jail.

How could he have been so stupid? Just like his mother always said, he didn't have the brain of an ant.

He got on the bus, closed the door, and squeezed his head between his hands. Stupid. Stupid. Stupid!

He deserved whatever he got. He attached his phone to a holder in the vent and started up the bus. GPS had worked right up until he turned onto Irfan Lane, so that meant his phone should work out on the main road, right?

He backed the bus onto the gravel road while something else niggled at him.

Nate and Lauren would pray about this, wouldn't they? Well, if they'd been him, they probably would have prayed before traipsing across Pennsylvania. Besides, it was too late now, wasn't it? He'd already made the idiot decision, so there was no going back.

Still, he glanced upward as he put the bus in drive and breathed out, "Help."

He reached the main road and checked his phone. Yes! Service! He pulled over on the shoulder and did a search for the campground. After finding the website, he made the call.

Someone answered before the first ring and finished. "Hunky Dory RV Park and Campground. How can we make your day?"

"Is there a Nate Brooks or Lauren Bauman there?"

Silence answered, followed by muffled background noises, then finally a familiar voice. "That you, Jet?"

"Lauren, it's good to hear your voice." He hoped, anyway.

"Where are you? What have you done?"

"I'm on my way back. Can I explain when I get there?"

A sigh came over the line. "I don't know. We just hung up with the police."

Chapter Twelve

So, he'd gone to meet his father.

Lauren sat on a wood bench and watched the road the purple bus should motor down any minute now. Nothing but birds flocking overhead. How was it fair that Jet had two living parents, but no loving mom and dad? No true home. And here she was, an orphan who'd been adopted—maybe not legally, but emotionally— by several families. She had no reason to be angry or afraid. She had everything she needed, and with that, even if she never had her own house, she'd always have a home to go to, a place she could call home. It had just taken her a long way to realize that.

"Any sign?" Nate came from behind her and handed over a lemonade.

"Nothing." She sipped at the ice-cold drink.

"Do you think he lied to get further away?" Nate sat beside her.

She stopped sipping, and the lemonade splattered on her T-shirt. Jet lying about coming back hadn't even occurred to her. He'd sounded sincerely contrite.

"What do you think?" Could it be, she'd been taken for a

fool again? It certainly wouldn't be the first time.

He shrugged. "There's not much we can do about it now. I'm gonna trust that he told the truth, but if he didn't, Uncle Ricky knows a good attorney."

She prayed it wouldn't come to that.

"Is that it?" Nate pointed up the road, at the sliver of a rooftop cresting the hill. But it was only a pickup.

"Nope." Every vehicle that came from that direction had raised their hopes, only to be dashed to the ground once again. "What about him staying on at Our Home?" Clearly, stealing a bus was breaking the rules, but Nancy also was one who applied common sense to every situation, and that didn't always mean a zero-tolerance policy.

"I don't know. This is sort of a biggie."

Lauren didn't disagree, but her heart still broke for Jet who was just trying to figure out how to piece together the broken shards of his life. If they deserted him now, would he ever pull himself together?

Would he allow God to shape him?

A rumble came from the opposite direction, and she and Nate jerked around.

The Draken!

Coming in the back way.

Thank you, Jesus!

She leapt up and jogged toward their parking spot. This was certainly one of those moments 1 Corinthians spoke about, in keeping no record of wrongs. Right now, Jet needed love, not discouragement. He'd had enough of that in his short life.

Nate and the bus beat her to the parking spot. She lifted a prayer that Nate would go easy on his friend. They were still friends, weren't they?

The door opened, and Jet trudged down the steps. His downcast eyes told her he was beating himself up again.

Nate met him silently, his hands ensconced in his back pockets. Tension radiated between the two men like the sun heating the desert.

That meant it was up to her to amend the situation. She stepped in front of Nate and wrapped her arms around Jet's shoulders. "I'm so glad you came back."

He stood rigid for what seemed like minutes, but then she heard a sniffle and he slouched in her arms. "I'm sorry, Lauren, for letting you down. And Nate, I'm sorry for taking your bus without asking or telling you where I was going. I keep messing up."

"Yeah. You do." Nate's voice was a growl. "But." His voice softened. "If you counted all the times I've royally messed up, you'd need a calculator just to keep track."

"But . . . " He pushed back from Lauren and looked around. "Where are the cops?"

"We told them we found you, and it was all a mistake."

"We?" Jet looked at Nate.

"Blame her." He motioned toward Lauren with his elbow.

Jet's head seemed to be on a swivel as he looked between the two siblings, his eyes drawn together, forming two distinct lines between his eyebrows. "This is what real love looks like, right?"

"Yeah." Lauren grinned and took the arms of both guys. "This is what you call love."

"Huh." Jet looked back at the bus, then at Lauren. "I want—I need—to know more."

Jet watched the bus head down the blacktop road, away from the campground. He hoped he hadn't ruined their day completely and that they'd enjoy the tour of Hershey. Needing to digest what Nate and Lauren had told him about their faith, he was in no mood for the tour. Besides, he had to make a call to his counselor. Casey was not going to be happy.

Once the bus was out of sight, Jet followed a gravel path to the beach. The water was nowhere near warm enough for swimming, yet even in the early evening families and sunbathers filled the area.

He couldn't talk to Casey here. So, he strode along the shoreline, past a copse of trees, and he kept walking until the sights and sounds of civilization were far behind him.

He pulled his phone from his pocket and scrolled until he found Casey Martin - Counselor in his contacts. He held his finger above the name but didn't press.

Counselor . . .

One of the Bible verses Lauren had highlighted in her Bible called Jesus a Wonderful Counselor. But how did one have a counseling session with Someone you couldn't hear or see? Nate and Lauren would tell him to pray, which Lauren described as a two-way conversation.

That made no sense to him.

Still, he looked up at the sky clear of clouds and said, "Do You really hear me? Do You really love me?"

A two-way conversation meant that someone spoke back. Ha! Like that would happen. Jet refused to say another word until God actually answered, so he sat down in the grass, closed his eyes, and cleared his mind.

He didn't hear God's voice, but rather water lapping up on shore, birds communicating mating calls, newborn leaves dancing on the trees.

Further off, he heard families laughing, playing.

A gentle breeze whispered across his face and toyed with his hair.

The fragrance of lilacs and other spring flowers filtered past his nose.

And the warmth of the just-setting sun embraced him like a blanket fresh from the dryer.

Goosebumps broke out on his arms, and tears leaked from his eyes. He'd read in Lauren's Bible about how the mountains and hills sang and the trees clapped their hands. It hadn't made sense.

Then.

But now . . .

Now he understood.

Now he felt in his bones, that he was loved.

Now he believed.

Chapter Thirteen

*W*hile the guys entered Sheila and Ricky's home below to grab a snack and beverage, Lauren carried the final box up the stairs to her apartment. *Her* apartment. Not Nate's home. Not the school dorm. This place was hers to decorate however she wanted. It was hers to live in. But, was it home?

She stopped at the top of the steps, set down the box, and glanced around. The small kitchen was straight ahead, with a large window overlooking the front yard. A drop-leaf table with two chairs sat between the kitchen peninsula and a sofa, creating the feel of a separate dining area. A cozy bathroom was squeezed between the living room and her bedroom. The bedroom also had a small nook, perfect for a small office area, that overlooked a park-like backyard.

The door at the bottom of the stairs opened and shut, followed by the patter of little feet hustling up behind Lauren, along with heavier footsteps of an adult.

She turned just in time to snatch little Susanna from the steps. Sheila and Ricky's toddler had more energy than libraries had books. "Caught ya!" She drew Susanna into a hug before the child squirmed to the floor while grasping a rubber snake in her hand.

"I 'scaped." Susanna raced to the couch and jumped up on it.

"Susanna Marie." Sheila's don't-you-dare-cross-me voice came from behind Lauren, and the child immediately sat still. Sheila sighed and stopped beside Lauren. "You would think that God would have given Richard and me a more laid-back child. This one's going to have me worn out before I reach forty-two."

Lauren laughed. "And I see she has a new pet."

"Don't get me started. That child loves anything reptile. Richard has threatened to get her a real snake. Over his dead body."

Oh, she'd missed this family! And to think, now she'd get to see them almost every day! "When you need a break, you know who to call."

"We will definitely be taking you up on that." Sheila gestured to the couch. "Would you mind keeping an eye on Zanna Belle for a few minutes? Richard has asked me to join him in a meeting."

Sorrow swept through Lauren's body. "About Jet's future with Our Home, right?" When Jet took the bus without permission, he'd pretty much cemented getting booted out of Our Home.

Sheila nodded.

And Lauren sighed. She had to speak up for him. He deserved a second chance, right? "Before you go, can I speak on Jet's behalf?"

"Absolutely." Sheila led the way to the sofa and picked

up her daughter, who immediately wriggled like a snake from Sheila's arms onto the floor.

Lauren sat beside Sheila and stared straight ahead at a blank wall waiting for her to decorate. "When I first realized who Jet was, I had a panic attack."

"And that's when you called me."

"Right. And like always, you helped me through that, but I wasn't expecting what happened next." Lauren's gaze flickered to the floor where Susanna wriggled on her tummy with her pet. "I became angry, and I treated Jet horribly. He didn't deserve it. He never even complained. Thing is, that's what he was used to growing up. That was how his mother and father treated him. He didn't have a chance to be anything but a bully until Nate picked him up and Our Home took him in. And despite how I treated him, he learned. And so did I."

Sheila put an arm around Lauren's shoulders and gave her a gentle squeeze. "When we moved that beautiful piano downstairs to this home, I was devastated by how out of tune it was. Then I listened, cringing, while the master tuner actually made it go further out of tune before making it sing. I've learned that's how God works sometimes. To mold us into the shape he's designed for us, sometimes he has to break us down further—put us way out of tune— before the Master tuner transforms us into something beautiful."

Lauren nodded, knowing that was what had happened on the bus ride. "I realized I'd held onto my anger all these years and had never forgiven him and denying him forgiveness made me an ugly person. Being around him was like holding a mirror to myself. I didn't like what I saw."

"You were—still are—always will be—a work in progress."

"I'm realizing that. And I'm seeing firsthand how God shapes people. Jet, in spite of how I treated him, was eager to learn about God, and he was starving to know what real love is. He made a mistake at the end, but I don't know that I can fault him. All he wanted was his father's love."

Sheila pressed a kiss to her forehead like a loving mother would. Something Jet never had. "I'll be sure to pass that along."

"Thank you. I also . . . " This was the part she really didn't understand. "After all this, I sort of like him."

"Sort of?"

"Yeah, well . . . " She shrugged and poured out her mixed feelings, then together they prayed for wisdom.

Jet sat straight as a carpenter's level in the Brooks' home office, his fingers fidgeting on his lap, while waiting for Our Home's chairman and vice-chair to arrive. Jet had met Mr. and Mrs. Brooks earlier while bringing Lauren's belongings to her apartment above this home, and they seemed like a pretty cool couple. Still, he was perspiring more than he had when fixing The Draken on Chicago's freeway.

Working with powerful women and men wasn't an issue—he was used to that—but these two were different. They were people he wanted to please.

"I'll be right in." A female voice spoke from behind him. Sounded like she was just outside the office. "Lauren has your daughter."

"And the snake?" A male voice—sounded like Mr. Brooks—asked with humor in his voice.

"Go do your job, mister."

And then there was laughter. The teasing. He'd learned that was love too. Someday, he hoped to experience that with a family of his own.

"Good afternoon, Jet." Mr. Brooks strode past Jet and sat behind the desk. "Thank you for waiting."

"No problem." Hopefully, he was done making problems for these people.

"I spoke with Nancy earlier today." Mr. Brooks set a manila file on his desk and looked over at Jet, unsmiling. Jet's file from Our Home? The man's eyes had a warmth to them that Jet rarely saw from those who frequented boardrooms.

Still, Jet gulped, unable to verbally respond. For the first time he could remember, he had something good going for him, and he'd flushed it away with an idiotic decision.

"Also, Lauren and Nate have put in a very good word for you." Mr. Brooks folded his hands on top of the file. "Even so, Nancy, Sheila, and I agree that it's in Our Home's best interest for you not to return."

It was the response he'd expected, but disappointment

weighed down his shoulders. Like his mother always told him, he was a screw-up. "I understand."

"I don't think you do, son." Mr. Brooks leaned back in his chair then gestured to a wall off to his right that was covered in pictures. The words "Our Family" were painted on the wall's center, and pictures surrounded the words. Some faces he recognized as Our Home residents, some were people who worked or volunteered there, but most were unfamiliar. In each photograph, the subject was smiling or even laughing. Not that fake smile-when-you-say-cheese kind of smile, but the genuine kind that showed in a glint in the eyes, the tilt of the head, and the pride of their stature.

"Each one of those young people found a home at Our Home." He stood and walked over to the wall and gestured to a picture. "Not all stayed, unfortunately. As you know, it's up to the individual. No one is forced to stay."

"But some of us choose by our actions." If only Jet could take back his horrid choice. Tell his father, "No!" and go on that date with Lauren.

"True, but if we can help it, no one leaves without having other options."

Other options? For the first time since he'd run off with The Draken, hope's ember was lit. "I'd like to know more, Mr. Brooks."

He grinned and waved someone into the office. "Around here, people call me Ricky, and my wife goes by Sheila."

Mrs. Brooks—Sheila—came in and gave her husband a kiss on the cheek. "And to some of us, he's Richard." She offered her hand to Jet while her husband returned to his seat. "I just came from speaking with Lauren."

He gulped. What had Lauren told her? About his behavior at the ballgame? At the campground? This couldn't be good.

Sheila wheeled another chair beside Ricky. "She tells me you made quite the impact on her. A positive impact."

Positive? Really? "I don't know about that." Beyond the fact that he'd proven he hadn't grown up since middle school.

"We do." She shared a glance with her husband. "We know that you're determined to put your anger issues behind you, which isn't an easy thing."

No, no it wasn't. He shrugged. "Guess I'm a work in progress."

"As are we all." She folded her hands on the desk. "And Nate mentioned earlier that you recently became a believer. A Christian."

"Yes, ma'am, but—"

"Please, no *ma'ams* around here."

"And she means it." Ricky shot her a sideways grin.

"I've got a ton to learn yet." And read. He'd only had time to read a few chapters of Genesis and Matthew so far.

"Good. Then you'll fit right in around here, if you're interested."

He blinked and then stared at the couple. "I don't understand."

Ricky opened the file in front of him and pulled out a page. "Our Home was born three-and-a-half years ago because my wife had the chutzpa to take a homeless teen into our home. We've learned that all these kids needed a healthy dose of love, and love looks different for each person. It's about meeting people where they are, just like Jesus does."

"Okay." His hands resumed their fidgeting.

"Nate, Lauren, and Nancy also raved about your working magic with engines," Ricky said. "Is that something you're interested in pursuing career wise, or would you prefer to keep it a hobby?"

"Uh, well, I hadn't considered it before staying at Our Home, but now I'm very interested. I've always been in the property management biz."

"Where I presume you learned to fix a thing or two, like my husband does."

"I guess." Actually, fixing things had always been his favorite part of the job at TC Property Management. No one ever called him stupid or idiot when he turned on their heat or fixed their plumbing.

Ricky handed him several pieces of paper, the top of which was an ad for Thurk Auto Service. "A friend of mine has his own auto repair shop and is always looking for good workers."

"But I'm not skilled yet—"

Ricky held up his hand. "He's looking for someone to apprentice with him while they attend school. Can I recommend you to him, or would you prefer to return to Minneapolis?"

Jet sat numb, trying to digest what the man across from

him was saying. "You mean, I could move here to go to trade school?"

"There would be an interview with William first—he's the owner of Thurk Auto Service—but we tend to think alike. If that works out for you, we can hook you up with housing. Or if you'd prefer to return to Minneapolis, I have connections there as well. I believe you know Gregg from Starr Motors."

"That's who I worked with at Our Home."

"He also put in a good word for you, called you an engine whisperer."

Jet rarely cried, but tears were threatening now. No one had ever done anything like this for him before. No one had ever seen his potential, only his weaknesses. He'd be a fool to turn down this opportunity, not only for a job he might enjoy, but to move here and get out from under his mother's giant thumb. Her reach extended over the entire Minneapolis-St. Paul area and deep into the suburbs. Maybe, just maybe, if he stayed in New York, Lauren could forget what he'd done to her all those years ago.

"I'd like to talk with Mr. Thurk."

"Smart move." Ricky gathered his papers together and inserted them into the manila file. "He's available tomorrow morning before you head back with Nate. If you get the position, we'll fly you out here."

Tingles shot from his neck down to his fingers, but these weren't tension-related. "Why are you doing this for me? If you knew all the things I've done. What I did to Lauren . . . "

"Each one of them is covered by God's mercy." Ricky

gripped his wife's hand. "I've been forgiven of the most heinous acts. How can I not extend that same mercy to others?"

"Thank you." Those two words didn't seem adequate for the gift he'd been given, but that was all he could think to say. He braced his hands on the armrests and prepared to stand. "Is that all?"

"Not quite." Sheila's face took on a sternness, telling Jet he didn't want to cross her. She gestured to the living room where he heard someone playing piano. "There's a young woman out there who says the two of you have unfinished business. She would like to speak with you alone."

Oh, boy. Just like that, perspiration burst out on his body. He and Lauren hadn't spoken about their non-date. Honestly, he'd been too afraid to broach the subject. Was that what she wanted to talk about?

Sure, she'd forgiven him for all his mess-ups this past week, but that didn't mean she was still interested in him.

But more so, after his conversation with God last night, Jet was no longer certain of his feelings.

Someone cleared their throat, and Jet startled. He looked across the desk at the man who didn't know him at all yet had offered him a new future. His mouth had drawn into a hard line, and his eyes had lost their warmth.

Jet shivered.

"That young woman out there." Ricky pointed beyond the door. "She's like a daughter to me and to Nate's dad. You mess with her, you answer to us."

"And to me." Sheila crossed her arms.

"And to Nate." Jet swallowed hard.

"And Nate." Ricky repeated.

How wonderful for Lauren that she was loved so fiercely, but he couldn't promise there would be no broken hearts. His or Lauren's. "I'll do my best."

Ricky nodded. "Then I recommend you go see what she wants." He offered his hand, which Jet took.

Then he walked from the room while silently lifting a single word: "Help."

Lauren sat at Sheila's baby grand. Like at Our Home, the words "Love will always be our home" were stenciled on the wall above the instrument. Susanna climbed up on Lauren's lap, and the child immediately began pounding on the keys. With her pet snake. Yep, Sheila and Ricky were going to have fun with this toddler.

And Lauren would be right here witnessing that growth.

Amidst Susanna's poundings, Lauren started playing a song her dad had loved, one that mimicked the words above the piano, "Love Will Be Our Home."

Those words were true. Home wasn't the walls surrounding you or the roof over your head, but rather the love found inside those walls, which was what Our Home strived to bring to the residents—the family members living there.

She'd finally arrived home. Yes, she'd taken a long, bumpy route to get here—learning she had anger issues nearly as deep as Jet's had been a painful thing to face.

Amazing how freeing the words "I forgive you" were, for both the giver and the receiver. With all her emotions stuffed down inside, it was no wonder she hadn't felt at home since her father died.

"Sounds like our daughter's going to be the next Lorie Line." Sheila came up behind Lauren and scooped her squirming daughter away.

"I play pinano."

"How about we go outside and find some snakes instead?" Ricky stole his daughter from Sheila and set her on the floor. "Your big cousin Nate's out there."

"I wuv Nate!"

"He loves you too, Zanna Belle."

While Susanna raced for the outside door, Sheila cuffed her hands on her hips and skewered Ricky with an icy glare. "If one of those creatures finds its way into our house . . . "

"You'd blame me?" He slapped a hand to his chest, his mouth agape, and his eyes twinkling.

Sheila poked him in the chest. "You've been warned."

He grinned and offered his arm. "Then I recommend you join me to keep all of us in line."

"If that's what it takes." She took his arm and looked back at Lauren, smiling and shaking her head. "See what I have to put up with?"

Yep she did. Love. Someday, maybe, Lauren would find a guy to love her just as much.

She resumed playing the master-tuned piano and heard someone clear their throat behind her. And someday she'd finish this song. Keeping her fingers poised above the keyboard, she glanced to her left.

Jet stood rubbing his hands over his jeans. Uh-oh. Did that mean he had bad news? If she'd been kinder to him at the first part of the trip, would that have made a difference in his choices? Maybe he wouldn't have felt compelled to take the bus yesterday.

"Mind if I have a seat?" He nodded to the empty space beside her.

But that was too intimate for her, so she gestured to the sofa near the windows overlooking the front yard.

He took one end of the couch, and she the other. Perfect.

His hands continued rubbing on his jeans as if he were trying to stoke a fire, and he kept his face angled toward the floor.

She'd be the one to break the silence. "I learned something last night. About your name."

"My name?" His gaze flitted up to hers.

"Jethro. Do you know what it means?"

He slouched and stared at the floor. "No idea." He mumbled. "It was my grandpa's name, and my mother always said he was a loser. Then there was the idiot on *The Beverly Hillbillies* TV show. Mother always said the name fits."

"Well your name does fit you, but it certainly doesn't mean loser or idiot." She glanced around the room and found a Bible on an end table. "It's from the Bible."

"Really?"

"Um-hum." She thumbed through the pages until she

found what she wanted. "Jethro was Moses' father-in-law. You know who Moses was?"

"The Ten Commandments dude?"

She laughed. "Yep. That's him. Anyway, Jethro was a priest and an upstanding man. The name has Hebrew origins and means excellence and abundance. So, yes, the name fits you perfectly."

Finally, Jet sat up straight. "You mean that?"

"A hundred percent."

He grinned, but as quickly as it appeared, the grin vanished. "If I were so *excellent*, I wouldn't have to be kicked out of Our Home."

Unbidden tears glossed her eyes, and she looked around for a tissue. "I'm so sorry, Jet." Now what would happen to him? Would he return to his old life?

He held out his hands, giving the stop signal. "But it's okay. I have new options."

"You do?" Hope dried those tears faster than a tissue would have.

He told her about the opportunity at Thurk Automotive, and his eyes glinted with a sheen she'd never seen in them before. "If everything works out, I'll likely be staying out east."

"That's wonderful news!"

"You think so?" His gaze finally met hers.

"I can't think of a better profession for an engine whisperer." She reached over and touched his hand. "I'm happy for you."

She started pulling her hand back, but he grasped it. "I

have a question."

Goosebumps raced up her arms, and this time, she was the one avoiding his gaze.

"I know we have a not-so-good history together, but I was wondering if you'd be willing to put that behind us and maybe start over again? This time as friends?"

Friends? Why did that word disappoint? She barely knew the guy, and most of the time she'd spent with him, she'd been angry. Still, he'd made such an amazing turnaround this week. As had she. But with his past and anger issues and new faith, logic told her being friends-only was the smart way to go. "I'd like that."

"So, it's true that love doesn't keep a record of wrongs."

"Real love doesn't. God's love doesn't. I can't either."

She'd taken the long way home to realize that. A week-long road trip that taught her that love was what truly defined a home.

Dear Reader,

Thank you for joining me on this road trip with Lauren, Jet, and Nate. Keeping no record of wrongs is showing real love, but as we learn from Lauren, forgiving isn't always easy. When we do forgive, though, healing becomes possible.

If you enjoyed Long Way Home, *please consider sharing a book review, telling other readers why you liked this story. The review doesn't have to be long or eloquent, just honest. Go here to review:* https://www.amazon.com/dp/B07C1RRMWS/.

You'll find further inspiration and encouragement on The Potter's House Books website and by reading other books in this uplifting series. Find all the books on Amazon and on The Potter's House Books website.

Book 1: *The Homecoming* by Juliette Duncan
Book 2: *When it Rains* by T.K. Chapin
Book 3: *Heart Unbroken* by Alexa Verde
Book 4: *Long Way Home* by Brenda S. Anderson
Book 5: *Promises Renewed* by Mary Manners
Book 6: *A Vow Redeemed* by Kristen M. Fraser
Book 7: *Restoring Faith* by Marion Ueckermann
(pre-order May 22, 2018)
Books 8 – 21 to be advised

To be notified of all new releases, join my email list at BrendaAndersonBooks.com/Subscribe. As a Thank You for subscribing, you will receive a FREE copy of Coming Home, *a Coming Home Series short story.*

Thank you for joining me on this writing journey!

In Him,
Brenda

Acknowledgements

Thank you to the six other Potter's House Books authors who welcomed me into the fold. It's an honor writing alongside all of you!

Thank you to Patti Hierl and Lorna Seilstad for helping me understand diabetes. Any mistakes are my own.

Thank you Stacy Monson, Lorna Seilstad, and Shannon Taylor Vannatter, my amazing critique partners, who always take my ugly-duckling early drafts and help mold them into swans!

Thank you, Gayle Balster, for always daring to read my first drafts and offering encouragement!

And thank you to my daughter, Sarah, for helping me make my twenty-something characters actually sound like twenty-somethings.

Thanks to my sons, Bryan and Brandon, whose writing aspirations encourage me to keep writing.

Special thanks to my husband who not only puts up with my writing career but is my number one cheerleader!

Thanking God always feels inadequate. To think the Creator of the universe gave me the gift of creating new worlds, if only on paper! What a privilege!

Other Potter's House Books

Find all the Potter's House Books at:
http://pottershousebooks.com/our-books/

Find all of Brenda S. Anderson's books at:
www.BrendaAndersonBooks.com/books

Coming Home Series

Praise for the Coming Home Series

"Anderson tackles family dynamics, tough issues, and gritty realism in her Coming Home series. From special needs babies to abortion and homelessness, you'll root for her authentic characters as they face real life struggles."
— Award-winning author, **Shannon Taylor Vannatter**

"... heartfelt, heart-wrenching fiction at its best, exploring relationships and family, love, faith and forgiveness in fresh, life-changing ways. I see myself in these endearing, enduring characters, their weaknesses and struggles and hard-won triumphs."
— **Laura Frantz**, author of *A Moonbow Night*

"Anderson thrusts her readers into the gritty underbelly of family life and she doesn't mince words or shy away from the difficulties that complicate relationships. The reoccurring themes of grace and restitution are delivered with heart-wrenching honesty. These compelling stories celebrate the joys and sorrows of ordinary living with an extraordinary God."

— **Kav Rees**, BestReads-kav.blogspot.com

Where the Heart Is Series

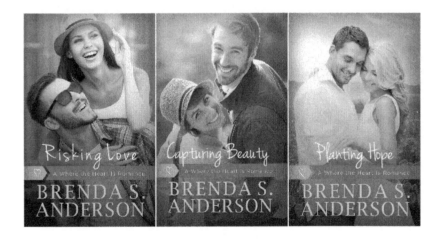

Praise for the Where the Heart Is Series

"*Risking Love* is a touching story of love and loss - and risking your heart! I can't wait to read the next in the series!"

—**Regina Rudd Merrick**, author of *Carolina Dream*

"Brenda does a great job bringing us into the story, capturing our attention and keeping it till the end. I read the first book in this series and look forward to the next. I highly recommend *Capturing Beauty* – it's an inspiring story of second chances and new perspectives!"

—**Angela D. Meyer**, author of *Where Hope Starts*

"*Planting Hope* is a lovely wrap-up to the Where the Heart Is series. The strength, or lack thereof, of a family unit has a profound impact on all of its members. Brenda Anderson expertly illustrates that in this story, and all of her books, as she deals honestly with the idiosyncrasies of families – the good, bad, and ugly. *Planting Hope* is about the hope God plants deep in our hearts, and the lengths we'll go to for those we love."

—Award-winning author, **Stacy Monson**, author of *Open Circle*

Brenda S. Anderson writes gritty and authentic, life-affirming fiction. She is a member of the American Christian Fiction Writers, and is Past-President of the ACFW Minnesota chapter, MN-NICE, the 2016 ACFW Chapter of the Year. When not reading or writing, she enjoys music, theater, roller coasters, and baseball (Go Twins!), and she loves watching movies with her family. She resides in the Minneapolis, Minnesota area with her husband of 30 years, their three children, and one sassy cat.

Connect with Brenda

Email: Brenda@BrendaAndersonBooks.com

Website: www.BrendaAndersonBooks.com

Newsletter: http://brendaandersonbooks.com/subscribe/

Facebook: facebook.com/BrendaSAndersonAuthor/

Twitter: twitter.com/BrendaSAnders_n

Pinterest: pinterest.com/brendabanderson/

Goodreads: goodreads.com/BrendaSAnderson

BookBub: bookbub.com/authors/brenda-s-anderson